"You're one hell of a

She looked up at him, ran her fingers over the strong lines of his face. She thought of all his kindnesses. With Hobo. With the vets. With the children he'd met today.

"Ditto," she said. "I mean, if I substitute *you* for *me*, and *woman* for *man* and..."

She stopped abruptly and analyzed what she'd just said. "That doesn't make sense, does it?"

He chuckled. "Yeah, it does." He leaned down and his lips trailed kisses down her face. Heat was growing between them again, their eyes locked on each other. "I would love to take you to bed," he said, "but it's too soon for that, isn't it?"

She didn't answer. She didn't have an answer. Her body was betraying her. Maybe she could steal a few days of pleasure.

"You should go," he said softly, "before we do something we both might regret."

Dear Reader,

Welcome to Covenant Falls and its bevy of veterans who make a difference.

Covenant Falls is a sleepy small town nestled next to the mountains in Colorado. In recent years, it's had an influx of veterans who have banded together to help the town and other veterans.

Former ranger medic Ross Taylor, now a physical therapist, is asked by a former army buddy to help with New Beginnings, a six-week Horses for Heroes equine therapy program for veterans with PTSD and other problems associated with combat.

I fell in love with him as he grumpily rescues an injured dog on his way to Covenant Falls. But he has demons of his own, and it takes the veterans he came to help—along with a pretty innkeeper, a grungy dog and a cantankerous cat—to help him heal, as well.

In researching this story, I found numerous privately sponsored Horses for Heroes programs throughout the country. They vary in length and services. Some are as intensive as the one portrayed in *Home on the Ranch: Colorado Cowboy*. Others range from free horseback riding at a ranch or farm to a series of long-weekend stays with counseling sessions. If you are interested in learning more or know someone who might benefit from such a program you can simply look up Horses for Heroes or equine therapy programs for vets.

Happy reading,

Patricia

HOME *on the* RANCH
COLORADO COWBOY

— ✛ —

PATRICIA POTTER

⬥ HARLEQUIN® HOME ON THE RANCH

Recycling programs
for this product may
not exist in your area.

ISBN-13: 978-1-335-83490-4
ISBN-13: 978-1-335-04189-0 (Direct to Consumer edition)

Home on the Ranch: Colorado Cowboy

Copyright © 2019 by Patricia Potter

H HARLEQUIN®

Printed in U.S.A.

™ www.Harlequin.com

USA TODAY bestselling author **Patricia Potter** has been telling stories since the second grade, when she wrote her first story about wild horses. She always knew writing was her future, but storytelling was diverted when curiosity steered her into journalism.

Storytelling, though, won out, and her first book—a historical set during the Civil War—was bought by Harlequin. She has since written more than seventy books and novellas, ranging from historical to suspense to contemporary romance.

She has received numerous writing awards, including the *RT Book Reviews* Storyteller of the Year Award, the Career Achievement Award for Western Historical Romance and Best Hero of the Year. She is a seven-time RITA® Award finalist and a three-time Maggie Award winner.

She is a past president of the Georgia Romance Writers, River City Romance Writers and Romance Writers of America.

Books by Patricia Potter

Harlequin Superromance

Home to Covenant Falls

The Soldier's Promise
Tempted by the Soldier
A Soldier's Journey
The SEAL's Return

Visit the Author Profile page
at Harlequin.com for more titles.

Dedicated to the Horses for Heroes programs and others who serve our veterans.

Chapter 1

The lump on the side of the road was out of place.

Despite his speed on the nearly empty two-lane road that connected nowhere with nowhere, Ross Taylor noticed everything on and around whatever path, trail or road he traveled. It was instinctual after years in the Middle East, where carelessness often meant death.

He slowed his Harley as he neared the lump. He was familiar with lumps, bumps, anything out of place. He treated them with respect. And caution. Even in the States.

He was almost even with the lump when he recognized the object as a dog. It lifted its head at the noise and then tried to move. *Dammit*. From the way it tried to drag itself, he knew the animal was in pain. And terrified. He knew the signs only too well. The dog was probably dumped by some jerk that had to know that few—if any—people used the road.

He should have known this trip was a bad idea. He hadn't wanted to go back to ranch country. Too many memories haunted him to this day. But the request came from the one man he couldn't refuse.

Dammit. He was already late for his appointments in Covenant Falls. A day late, in fact, and he didn't like being late. Ever. It had been drilled into him in the army. Equally as important, the sooner he finished the job, the sooner he could leave.

Still, he couldn't leave a living thing in pain. Swearing softly about people who abandoned dogs, he dismounted from his bike and approached the animal. It tried desperately to move away but was obviously hobbled by its injured leg.

As he knelt beside the dog, it shivered with fear and pain. Probably hunger and thirst, as well. It moved, or tried to move, and a soft moan came from its throat.

It was a nondescript dog on the smaller side of medium. It was so dirty he couldn't determine the color or breed but its large sorrowful brown eyes reflected fear and pain. Blood had stiffened the fur on its left leg. The fur was matted and full of burrs. Its scrawny body told him it hadn't had a meal in a long time. Probably dehydrated, as well.

"Hey, little guy," Ross said as he knelt down next to the animal and put a hand on its head. "Let's see what I can do for you."

The dog growled, obviously unsure of his intentions. Ross went to his bike's saddlebag and grabbed one of two squashed sandwiches he'd bought at the same gas station where he'd heard about the road and been given directions. He also dug out his canteen.

He sat down next to the animal, filled the top of the

canteen with a little water and held it out to the dog, which drank it frantically. When it was gone, Ross tore a small piece off the sandwich and placed it in front of the dog before inching back. He watched as the animal sniffed the offering and then gulped it down. It looked at him more hopefully.

"Recognize a friend now, huh, or is it desperation? I understand desperation." He kept his voice low and his hand gentle as he explored the dog's body. The animal yelped as he touched his rear left leg. His experience as a medic told him it looked as if he'd been hit by a bullet. The wound was in and out and looked as if was healing but there could be bone damage. He tried to soothe the dog, talking to him in a low calm voice as he finished his examination. Thank God, the abdomen appeared intact. The dog had probably been dumped and then someone else came along and used him for target practice or, worse, it had been the dumper.

"Stay here," he ordered although he knew the words were nonsense to the dog. He gave the dog a few more swallows of water. He wanted to give him more food, but he feared too much on an empty stomach would make him sick.

What in the hell was he going to do now? He couldn't leave him here. He checked his cell phone. No signal.

According to his map the next town on his route was probably about fifty miles away. And it was small. Unlikely to have a veterinarian or an animal rescue facility.

But the dog was looking at him with what Ross thought must be hope. He tried to get up on three legs, stumbled and landed back in a heap.

Ross couldn't leave him here. The dog needed more

medical care than he could provide. He needed a vet as soon as possible.

Ross was already late, delayed by his most recent client, who'd called at the last moment. He was in pain after a long session with Ross the day earlier. It had taken Ross half a day to convince the man it was common after the hard regimen the actor had insisted upon.

He'd been patient because Nick Mason recommended him to friends who had to be in top shape for their action films. They provided Ross the financial freedom to take the jobs he wanted to take. That included the pro bono work that had led him to today's destination.

He looked back at the dog. It trembled even as it stared up at him with both hope and fear.

"I won't abandon you," he said.

But how to manage this rescue? He was heading toward a town named Covenant Falls, where he'd been volunteered to help grow a Horses for Heroes program for troubled veterans. It wasn't his idea. He hadn't been on or near a ranch since he was ten years old. He was still haunted by memories of the night that changed his life, but he was indebted to the man who had volunteered him.

He gently ran his hand across the dog's back. "Not your problem," he told the dog. "I'll see you to a safe place."

How to do that was the problem. A motorcycle was not the best way to transport an animal, especially a wounded one. He took a quick mental inventory of his possessions. At least the dog didn't weigh much more than twelve pounds. At full weight he'd probably be another four or five pounds at the minimum.

Ross traveled light. He'd been an army medic before obtaining his physical therapy credentials and was used to traveling with a first aid kit and little else. His bike was his only transportation; he'd rigged a carrier on the luggage rack that held two waterproof canvas containers.

One included the first aid kit along with other items he considered necessary. The second bag contained the few clothes he expected to need, along with a kit for personal items such as razor and toothbrush. A lightweight sleeping bag and raincoat were strapped on top.

He took out the first aid kit and returned to the dog. Ross fed him another small piece of sandwich that now hid half an ibuprofen pill. He then washed the wound with the rest of the water from the canteen.

He found a small branch and used his pocketknife to carve a splint for the dog's leg, then wrapped it in bandaging from his kit. While the dog watched fearfully, Ross emptied the second canvas bag, stuffing clothes in the first one. He wrapped a long-sleeved denim shirt around his waist and made a nest of two T-shirts at the bottom of the canvas bag.

The problem, he knew, was keeping the dog safe inside the canvas bag until he could get him to a veterinarian. Sighing, he cut holes for air in the top and side of the canvas container he'd designed.

"I'm going to take care of you, buddy," he said, just as he had to soldiers who'd been wounded. Whether the dog was too exhausted or in too much pain to protest, he simply collapsed after Ross lifted him into the canvas bag. "Be warned, this is temporary only," Ross added. He needed to call the pup something. Hobo seemed to fit. He was on the side of the road, probably hoping for a ride. As if on cue, Hobo stuck his tongue out and licked his finger.

"Don't get any ideas," Ross said as he closed the basket. "This is a temporary situation only."

Dammit, he needed to get the dog to a vet. He doubted, though, he could find a veterinarian on the way, especially one that was open on late Saturday afternoon.

Although Covenant Falls was small and off the beaten track, it should have one, given the number of ranches he understood were in the area.

He tried to call the inn where he had reservations but there was no cell service. When he'd tried to call and change his booking earlier, the line was busy. He figured there was no problem—there would be plenty of rooms available.

He pondered the next move, but there really was no choice. No way could he leave the wounded mutt.

The dog was a survivor. Like him.

He mounted the Harley and took off. The sound of the engines prevented him from hearing any complaints from his small passenger who was probably terrified.

Susan Hall was uncharacteristically miffed. It was nearly eight o'clock on Saturday night and all but one of the Camel Trail Inn's guests had arrived. The only empty room belonged to a Ross Taylor who should have arrived yesterday. It looked as if he would be a no-show today, as well.

Ordinarily it wouldn't have bothered her. The inn usually had plenty of vacancies. In truth, too many. Tonight was different. It was the last weekend of the Covenant Falls historical pageant and it had drawn visitors from throughout the state. The inn was full with the exception of Room 20. She'd turned down paying guests last night and again tonight, including a very nice elderly couple who came for the pageant and didn't want to make a long drive at night.

She'd poured her heart and soul into making the inn self-sustaining. The two owners had given her an opportunity she never thought she would have after a very painful marriage and divorce. The inn became her refuge and future. She often worked twelve, fifteen hours a day, doing everything from taking reservations and helping in the kitchen to marketing and financials.

She didn't know how the inn would have survived without the pageant, which—during the summer—drew visitors to a town that was virtually unknown to the general public. The publicity about the pageant had grown, and visitors came from longer distances and were in need of lodging.

She glanced at her watch. She'd been here since six in the morning and sent her assistant, Judy, home an hour ago. Most of the guests were settled for the night and the young night manager could handle any guest requests.

She checked in the kitchen. Ethel Jones, a lifetime resident of Covenant Falls, had started as a part-time cook for the inn and now oversaw a small staff.

"Everything good?" she asked Ethel. The woman was supervising two more cooks and five very busy servers who were finishing with the early dinner service for those not attending the pageant. There was a second sitting at nine for those attending the event.

"Better than good," Ethel said. "Everything's going to schedule, thanks to our staff."

Susan left, her thoughts still on the last guest to arrive. Josh must want him here badly if he gave away one of the best rooms for two weeks. To cool off from the warmth of the kitchen, Susan walked outside and viewed the evening sky. The weather couldn't be better. Colorado often had early winters, but tonight's temperature was mild with a refreshing breeze and a clear sky. Perfect for the pageant.

She was sorry to see it end this year. Now that summer was over, occupancy at the inn would decline drastically. It was especially important now to bring in as many paying guests as possible. A two-night stay paid for a week's salary for an employee.

She returned to the inn to discover that Mark, the night manager, had arrived.

"You're early," Susan said.

"Judy told me you've been here all day," he replied. I thought you might want a meal in peace and some sleep."

"Good thought. Especially the sleep part."

"Any problems?" Mark asked.

"Mr. Taylor is a no-show again. A perfectly delightful older couple really needed a room but…"

As if on cue, the same couple, the Turners, entered the inn and headed toward the desk. Susan went over to them. "Hello again." She smiled. "I thought you were leaving after the pageant."

"We heard about the restaurant," the woman said. "Some people at the pageant said the food here was really good. We rushed over ahead of the crowd in hopes you could squeeze us in. We'll try to find a motel on the way home."

"I think I can manage an extra table," Susan said. "And I might be able to get you a room. A guest who had the reservation hasn't checked in yet and didn't arrive last night. If he doesn't appear by 10:00 p.m., you can have it."

It was a few minutes before nine now. The couple

looked at each other with hope. "Thank you," the woman said. "It's our anniversary."

"I hope we can make it special."

Susan took the couple over to Mark and explained the plan to him and then left the couple with him while she returned to the kitchen. "Can you fit another table in?" she asked Ethel. "It's an older couple who are celebrating an anniversary. They're from out of town."

"Sure can," Ethel said. "It'll be tight but I can arrange it."

"I'll send Mark to help."

"Okay to treat them to dessert?"

"Definitely," Susan said.

She returned to the desk, where Mark was still talking to the couple. "We're all set for dinner," she told them. "The dining room will open in a few minutes. Just check with Mark after dinner about the room."

She looked at the clock. Now that the pageant was over, they would be deluged with diners.

"Thank you so much," Margaret Turner said. "We'll be sure to tell everyone about the inn. I just love the name, Camel Trail Inn. I read in the program that camels really roamed this area. We want to come back and explore."

"We would love to have you," Susan replied sincerely. "There's a lot of history here. I hope the room works out." She would bet anything that Mrs. Turner was the type to spread the word about Covenant Falls. Her interest—and her husband's—was obvious.

She gave them directions to the small inn library where they could wait until the dining room opened, then turned back to Mark. "I think I'll take your suggestion and go home," she said. "Poor Vagabond is probably starving."

"What about you?"

She usually stayed late the last night of the pageant to hear the entertainment but the last few days had been frantic and she was exhausted. A glass of wine and a hot bath were critically needed and the inn was in good hands with Mark.

She walked the half mile to her small bungalow. Vagabond, a stray cat that took up residence outside her house until Susan finally surrendered and admitted the cat inside, was probably wondering who was going to fill her bowl tonight. Because she had a tendency to overeat, Susan rationed each meal.

She'd never been a cat person, but a dog wasn't practical with her schedule and, well, the darn cat had adopted her, not the other way around.

Vagabond greeted her with her usual indignant "Are you trying to starve me?" meow. Susan quickly filled her dish with cat food, then poured a glass of wine and investigated the contents of Ethel's care package. It was one of her favorites, a salad packed with different greens, pieces of steak and blue cheese crumbles.

After eating, she poured a second glass of wine for herself, found the book she'd been reading for what seemed like forever and slipped into a hot bubbly tub. Finding she was too tired to read, she put it down, sipped the wine and thought about the day.

The inn had reached the point of breaking even a year ago and was inching up in the profit column. She was happy with her job and even happier for Josh and Nate, the two owners who had taken a huge risk in building the inn and hiring her to run it.

She worried, though, about the no-show today. What if he did show up and they had to turn that couple away?

All she knew about Ross Taylor was he was connected in some way to Josh and Jubal's Horses for Heroes program. But he was obviously thoughtless. Rude. Unreliable.

She drained the glass of wine.

Chapter 2

Ross roared into the Camel Trail Inn at nearly midnight on Saturday.

The parking lot was filled. Completely filled. He groaned.

He should have tried calling again, but he'd been too busy worrying about the darn dog.

He was going to have to try to sneak Hobo inside. No self-respecting inn would accept him, even with Josh Manning's approval. Who in the hell would have thought an inn in a tiny little town would be this busy.

He parked the Harley near the entrance door in the "check in only" space.

The inn looked a lot more inviting than he thought it would. *Dammit*. He would have preferred the infamous Bates Motel at the moment. He realized he looked like trouble walking in. He was wearing a sweaty T-shirt, worn jeans and a well-weathered leather jacket. He had two days' bristle on his face and was accompanied by a half-starved mongrel. It didn't help that he was a big man. His size often intimidated people. And whoever was at the desk probably heard the approach of the Harley.

Josh Manning, his sergeant and a close friend for several years in the Middle East, would probably disown him although he was here at Josh's request.

He decided to leave the dog in the basket. He walked through the quiet lobby to a desk manned by a slender young man who looked as if he was still in his teens. The desk clerk looked up from a book as Ross approached.

Mark—identified from the pin on his shirt—put the book to the side and despite Ross's appearance said politely, "Can I help you, sir?"

Ross instantly admired his composure. "Sorry to disturb you," he said, looking at the book titled *Hotel Economics.* "Good read?" he asked.

The kid smiled. "Can't put it down," he replied with a grin, "for more reasons than one. I have a test coming up."

Ross grinned at the reply. "I'm Ross Taylor. I think I have a reservation. Sorry to be so late but there were unexpected delays and either there was no cell service or your phone was busy."

A concerned look replaced the smile. "I'm sorry, sir, but when we didn't hear from you yesterday or today we gave the room to an elderly couple who didn't want to drive a long way tonight."

Perfect! It suited the rest of the day. Everything that could go wrong, had. "Is there any place else? I've been on the road for fifteen hours."

"I'll check," Mark said. "You can wait in the library

just to the left. The seats are more comfortable. Can I get you something to drink or eat while you wait?"

Ross thought of the dog on the back of his bike. He probably shouldn't mention him at the moment. "A sandwich would be good."

The kid nodded and reached for the phone as Ross walked around the lobby. He couldn't really be angry. It was his fault. He should have tried harder to contact the inn, but damned if he knew what to do now.

He studied the interior of the inn. It had a lodge look to it. Beams overhead and paneled walls. Western paintings decorated the interior and a huge fireplace dominated one wall. There was a large coffee urn on a counter along another wall.

If the inn couldn't find something for him, he could call Josh Manning, but dammit, he hated to do that. He would never hear the end of it if he had to call for help in the middle of the night. Not to mention the pitiful shape of his temporary dependent.

The idea had been to arrive yesterday and relax today before meeting with Josh on Sunday. So much for relaxing. But that was before the client needed reassurance and before he found Hobo. He'd had to stop repeatedly to check on the little guy.

Ross tried to relax. He didn't care if a room wasn't ready or if something was broken, unless it was the shower.

After a long relaxing bath, Susan emerged from the tub, poured another glass of wine, and she and Vagabond settled down in bed. After tomorrow's checkout, the inn would be nearly empty. It was both a relief and a worry.

The lull would allow her to help at Jubal's ranch as a

volunteer in the Horses for Heroes program. Although the program was really Jubal's baby, Josh was 100 percent behind it, and the entire town was involved in one way or another. She was a minor cog, more of a confidence builder than an instructor.

Which brought her back to the missing guest. All she knew of Ross Taylor was he was an army buddy of Josh's and a physical therapist who would be involved in the vet program.

She decided not to think about him tonight. She picked up the book but the words seemed to blend together and her brain wouldn't stop working.

She put the book aside and turned out the light only to be jerked fully awake by her cell phone.

"Ah…we have a small problem." Mark's voice was tentative.

Bad vibes ran through her. Mark rarely let anything bother him and was excellent at solving problems on his own.

"What kind of problem?"

"The guy who was supposed to be here yesterday just showed up."

Susan immediately came to full alert.

"Any more good news?"

"He doesn't look happy that we don't have a room, and he's big. Really big." There was a note of wariness in his voice.

She looked at the clock. It was nearly twelve. This was the last thing she needed tonight, but he was her boss's guest. Maybe Josh could take care of him—but it was late, and she knew for a fact that his house was already overflowing with both human and animal inhabitants.

She didn't relish calling him at midnight and admitting she'd given away a room booked for an old friend of his.

It was her problem. She was the one who had decided to give away the room tonight. She ran through alternatives in her mind. There weren't any. The two bed-and-breakfast homes in Covenant Falls were full, as were motels within fifty miles.

Maybe he could stay at her house. She had the space and had used it once before when the inn was overbooked. But that was for a couple. Still, this Ross Taylor was a personal friend of Josh's. It wouldn't be different than a bed-and-breakfast for one night.

She gritted her teeth. She didn't much like the idea of a male in the cottage, especially a strange one. But she had three bedrooms and two baths and, knowing this week was going to be hectic, she'd cleaned thoroughly a week ago. She would decide after meeting him. She took a deep breath.

Mark was still on the phone. Waiting.

"I'll come over there," she said. "Give him a drink or food, or both. You can get something from the kitchen. I won't be more than fifteen minutes."

"Will do," Mark said. He sounded relieved.

Susan reluctantly left the bed, dressed quickly in jeans and a sweatshirt. She ran a comb through her hair and tied it back in a ponytail, then applied a dab of lipstick.

Vagabond jumped down from the bed, meowing displeasure at her sleep being interrupted.

Susan was out the door and on the road eleven minutes after the call. The inn was only half a mile away and she arrived two minutes later.

The parking lot was full and she parked her Jeep in the arrival area at the entrance, joining a dusty gigantic motorcycle. Whimpering sounds were coming from a small basket on the back.

Neither the motorcycle nor the noises were good signs.

She went inside. The lobby was empty except for Mark, who was looking anxiously toward the door.

"He's in the library," he said. "I raided the kitchen, gave him a beer, three sandwiches and two of tomorrow morning's cinnamon rolls."

"Three sandwiches?"

"He's rather…hungry."

"How did he react to not having a room?"

"Well, he didn't rant," Mark said. "He said it fitted in with the rest of the day. I don't think he meant it in a favorable way."

"I heard a dog whimpering on a motorcycle on my way in," she said.

"He didn't say anything about a dog."

"The bike couldn't be good for it," she said, her opinion of the newcomer plummeting every moment. Who would put a dog in a tiny space on the back of a motorcycle? If that motorcycle was Ross Taylor's, the dog did complicate things, especially if it was sick. She knew that Stephanie, their vet, probably wouldn't return until late tomorrow. And the fact that her would-be guest kept an animal in a small container on a noisy bike didn't improve her opinion of him. She didn't care for motorcycles or those who rode them. They all had a death wish.

"What are you going to do?" Mark asked.

"I haven't decided." She turned around and walked to the library. A large man sat facing the door. Only half of one of the three sandwiches remained. His beer was nearly gone, as well. No cinnamon rolls remained. He'd obviously been hungry.

"Mr. Taylor?"

He started to get up.

"No," she said. "Don't get up. Finish," she ordered.

"Yes ma'am," he said in a slightly amused voice, set-tling back in the seat while he finished the sandwich in two bites. Then he sat back. Waiting.

"I'm Susan Hall," she explained. "I manage the inn. I'm sorry your room isn't available, and I'm here to fix the problem." She had no idea how she was going to do that, especially now she was staring at him. Dammit, she was in trouble.

He looked like he'd just walked off a Western movie lot after a long day of fighting bad guys. He was ruggedly handsome with a tanned face and several days of beard. His face was arresting, strong. His eyes were steel gray and seemed to penetrate through her sudden confusion. His hair was sandy blond, not curly exactly but thick and tousled, probably by the motorcycle helmet that was on the table. His forearms were heavily muscled and his hands looked strong and capable.

He was tall. Probably six foot three or more. Not thick. She'd noticed when he started to stand that there was not an ounce of fat on him. You could even call him lean but it was all solid muscle. He would dwarf her five foot nine and one hundred and thirty pounds. Blood stained the T-shirt he wore. A well-worn leather jacket was spread askew in another chair as if just tossed there.

He was attractive in a raw masculine way. She usu-ally didn't respond to power and self-assurance, and he radiated it.

She mentally winced under his gaze. She definitely did not look her best. She had pulled her hair back in one long messy ponytail rather than the neat knot or French braid she usually wore during business hours. Her clothes were certainly not business-like. Outside of a bare dash of lipstick, she'd forgone makeup in her haste.

But now she had no idea what to do as he speared her with an expectant gaze, waiting for her to offer a solution.

My boss's friend.

He raised an eyebrow as if to ask, without words, why he didn't have a room and what in the devil was she going to do about it.

Then he put it in words. "The young man at the desk said there may be a problem with the room. I don't care what's wrong with it. I just need a bed and especially a shower."

She certainly had to agree with the latter statement. There was only one possibility, and she fought with herself before offering it. He may not be dangerous in a physical way, but she knew immediately he could be in other ways.

He did not look like any physical therapist she'd known. He looked fierce, impatient and expectant.

She studied him. He had several days of beard but it was more sexy than off-putting. Above all, there was something magnetic about him.

Most women's dream. My nightmare. He was, in fact, the kind of man who sent her running in the opposite direction. The kind that roared into town and left broken hearts in its wake.

Like her father.

Susan tried to explain. "I'm afraid we don't have anything, not even a closet. This is one of the few weekends we're sold out," she explained. "When you didn't check in or call by ten, we gave the room to an elderly couple who really needed it." She waited for an explosion.

"I tried to call," he explained in a cool voice, "but either the line was busy or I was in a no-cell-service area. I would have been more persistent had I known there was a problem."

Susan winced. She should have thought about that possibility. "I apologize," she said. "This is our busiest weekend of the year. I didn't realize the phones were clogged. I should have."

She changed the subject, hoping it would give her time to think. "I heard little whimpering noises coming from a motorcycle as I came in." It was a question.

"A dog," he said. "The little guy was sleeping when I came in. I found him injured on the side of the road. Someone obviously shot him and left him in the middle of nowhere." The anger in his voice grew as he spoke. "He was half-starved but moved when he heard the bike. Trying to scoot away on an injured leg. I would like to do some bodily damage to who did that to him." His voice deepened in anger. I tried to find a veterinarian. None were open. I'm hoping you have one here."

"We do. A very good one. I would call her now but she's on a search and rescue mission with her dogs. Hopefully, she'll be back tomorrow."

Ross nodded. "He's had a hard day. From his condition, it looks like he's had a lot of them. Maybe always."

Her opinion of her guest spiraled upward. "So that's why you were running late."

"That and a client who was in more pain after a workout than he expected and thought I'd damaged him permanently."

"Bad week, huh?"

He shrugged and asked abruptly, "Do you have anything at all?"

Guilt weighed on her. It was even heavier now than when she gave away his room. Although she'd truly wanted to help the older couple, she'd had no authority to make that decision. She should have considered the reasons he might be late instead of assuming he was a no-show.

Although he was sprawled across a chair, he was compelling. His eyes drilled into her. He hadn't smiled, but neither had there been anger. More like frustration, but even that was laid-back.

The conversation swayed some of her reservations. Despite his appearance, he seemed to be reasonable. More than reasonable, really, considering the circumstances. "I have, ah…a…possible solution," she started awkwardly, which was totally unlike her.

He raised an eyebrow and his mouth widened into a slow smile that took her breath away. "I'm listening," he said.

"I could wake up Josh Manning," she said, "but he has a full house. Five dogs, a cat, a couple of horses, a son and a pregnant wife."

The eyebrow arched a little higher. "In that order?"

She had to smile at that. "Not quite."

"Are we talking about the same Josh Manning?" he said. "He was pretty much a loner when I knew him."

"In the army, you mean?"

"What makes you think that?"

"You mean besides that tattoo on your arm, the watchful eyes, the way you sit. You look relaxed but you're also ready to leap straight out of that chair if necessary."

He raised an eyebrow. "You're pretty observant."

"You have to be, in this business. I've managed some properties in places not as safe and law-abiding as Covenant Falls." She grinned. "Also because Josh gave me some background on you. Military medic. Physical therapist. I'm aware of how difficult that program is."

"Tell me more about Josh," he said. "It's been years since I've seen him. The call from him came out of the blue. We served several tours together and he saved my ass more than once so I owe him."

"Oh, he was a real loner when he showed up here. Mad as could be at the world. But then he met Eve, the city manager, and her son. He and his partner built this inn. He and a former SEAL are spearheading the program that brings you here. But you'll learn all this later. I'm not sure of your role, though," she added cautiously.

"Josh wants me to look over the physical therapy program and determine how to improve it as far as physical fitness goes. I understand some of the vets are in poor physical condition when they arrive here. He also wants advice in opening it to physically disabled vets. But now I need a place to stay for both the dog and myself. Maybe a campground…"

"None around here with any amenities like showers," she said, and her defenses collapsed. He was obviously tired and worried about a dog that wasn't his. Couldn't be a serial killer. At least she didn't think so, and she could deal with anything less than that. She'd wanted to get a feel for him before she made the offer she'd been toying with. While he looked formidable, there was also patience. Probably more than she would have had in similar circumstances.

In those few seconds she made up her mind. "I have a cottage a half mile from here. There's an extra room and bath. You're welcome to it. Breakfast goes along with it."

She saw him glance at her empty ring finger. He hesitated. "What about your family…?"

"I live alone except for Vagabond," she said. "I've rented out rooms in the house before when the inn was full. More importantly, you're a friend of Josh and that goes a long way in Covenant Falls."

"Vagabond?" he asked with a raised eyebrow that made him look even more rakish.

"A freeloader," she said. "A cat."

"Isn't the offer a bit reckless?"

"Vagabond is very protective," she said.

An eyebrow rose again. "Are you sure?"

"About the cat?" She purposely misread his question. "Yep. She's a scrapper. Scared the wits out of me when I accidentally stepped on her tail. And," she added, "I know karate. For backup."

That produced the hint of a smile. "Warning taken."

"I also trust Josh and, therefore, I trust you."

He nodded. "In that case, I accept. You have no idea how much I want to clean up."

She looked at him, her gaze running over the stained clothes and rumpled hair. "I get that."

"That bad?"

"I've seen worse. We better go. Your dog was stirring when I came in."

"He's not my dog."

"Well, since he's in your possession, he is at the moment."

"I'm hoping your veterinarian can find Hobo a home."

"Hobo?"

"I had to call him something, and he hitched a ride with me."

"What prevents *you* from keeping him?"

He shrugged. "I'm not anywhere long and I travel on my bike. Obviously not the best life for a dog."

"No physical home?"

"Nope," he replied. "I like living without permanent walls."

"Why?" she asked. She scolded herself for being intrusive, but then he was staying at her home. Shouldn't she know something about him other than his friendship with her boss?

He shrugged. "No one can tear them down or take them away."

It was a cryptic answer that was intriguing, but his expression did not invite exploration.

"And you obviously travel light, too."

"I got used to it in the army. I discovered I really didn't need a lot of things. I like the freedom of not owning much. Nothing to lose or worry about."

"And when it rains and snows and sleets?"

"I find a cubbyhole and burrow inside."

She looked at his long, hard frame again stretched over the chair. Burrowing didn't seem like a good option to her. He'd need too large a cubbyhole.

She raised an eyebrow. "Okay," she surrendered. Obviously he was closing the door on that topic.

He hadn't left a crumb behind from his meal. He started to neatly stack the few dishes.

"Don't worry about that," she said. "The night manager will take care of it."

He shrugged. "Habit. I've been taking care of myself for a long time."

"You're in an inn," she said in a half-stern voice, "that takes pride in catering to guests."

He raised an eyebrow.

"Most of the time," she amended primly. "There are exceptions when the inn is not kept informed."

"Point taken," he said with the first real smile she'd seen. She got the impression he didn't do that often.

"I'll meet you at the door," she said. "I have to talk to my night manager first." She paused, then added, "Do you want to ride with me or follow on the motorcycle?"

"The bike," he said. "Everything I own is on it. But I have to warn you, the dog is a little...dirty."

She wondered if the dog looked as disreputable as her guest did at the moment. His lips turned up at the corner as if he knew exactly what she was thinking. It was unnerving.

"He can get a bath at my house. I'll grab a few items from the kitchen." She veered off toward the front desk as he waited. She was back in minutes with a box. "Okay, let's go."

Chapter 3

On the drive to her house, Susan couldn't help but wonder if her invitation was the brightest idea she'd ever had, especially when she heard the loud sound of the motorcycle following behind her.

She was used to Covenant Falls and its neighborly ways and generous hearts. Everyone helped everyone else, and all the veterans who'd arrived in the past three years had proved to be of the same mold. If they weren't when they arrived, they certainly were *after* arriving.

She was happier in their ranks than any time in her previous adult life. They were all in this together, and "this" was growing the town while leaving its unique character intact. In the process her own life had changed. She owed that to Josh. As far as she was concerned, he could do no wrong.

This guy was his friend. A fellow Ranger. She'd had

her doubts when she first saw him. He looked more like an outlaw than a physical therapist. She'd learned, though, that the incoming veterans turned out to be great guys, and she warned herself not to prejudge the newest one.

She also knew that if he got out of line, Josh and the others would make him very, very sorry, friends or not. Among the vets, she was treated like a sister, and that was great. Growing up, she'd been a tomboy who was more comfortable among boys than girls. She'd been equal among them in racing horses and some sports.

She'd also been perfectly honest when she'd told Ross Taylor she knew karate. She'd been vulnerable once. She intended never to repeat that mistake.

So she felt safe enough. Physically, at least. She wasn't so sure about the rest of her emotions. It had been a long time since any guy had sparked her interest. She'd been too badly burned. Yet despite the rough appearance of her surprise guest, she was intrigued. A physical therapist that lived on a motorcycle. A warrior who helped people heal.

No more time to question your decision. It took only minutes to arrive at her cottage. She'd bought it for a fraction of its worth when the owner died without heirs and the property reverted to the bank.

She glanced in the rearview mirror. Ross Taylor was right behind her. She parked in front of the house and signaled him to go into the unattached garage, which she'd left open in her rush to the inn.

She tried not to think about her elderly neighbors and his bike's thunderous approach. Most of them would be asleep but then there was the morning to consider.

One of the joys of a small town was everyone knew

everyone. One of the problems with a small town was everyone knew everyone's business. She shrugged. She could explain later.

Susan left the Jeep on the street, met Ross Taylor in the garage and turned on the interior light. She watched as he unbuckled two bulging saddlebags from the front of the bike and threw them over his left shoulder, then unbuckled one of two large containers from a platform at the rear of the bike.

He opened one and lifted out the scruffiest-looking dog she'd ever seen. It was small—about the size of a small terrier—and its leg was bandaged. The animal was brown, but she suspected several layers of dirt had darkened its color. At least one flea was obvious, and Susan knew their relatives were hiding in the thick, matted fur.

The dog stared back at her with suspicion.

She reached out a hand. The dog flinched and uttered a warning growl.

"He's not sure who is friend and who is foe," Ross said. "I think he's seen some rough times." He looked up. "Is there part of a lawn he could sprinkle for a few minutes?"

"Sure," she said. "Pick any place in the front yard, then we'll manage a bath." *We?* Did she really say that?

Her guest nodded and gently—for a big man—lowered the dog to a green spot next to the garage. The dog didn't waste time. He awkwardly lifted a leg while balancing on the two good legs and the one with a cast.

The dog looked like a combination of more than a few breeds. Even under the best of circumstances she doubted he would be handsome. His fur was long and matted and he definitely had an odor about him. His eyes were a little clouded. His toenails looked as long as an eagle's talons. He was also very thin.

Ross Taylor gave her a wry smile. "He looked even worse a few hours ago. Some water and food has helped."

"I'm surprised he did well in that basket."

"I have some mild sedatives in my first aid kit and gave him one. He slept most of the way. We made stops for water and for him to relieve himself."

"You said you found him on the road?"

"Some bastard shot him and left him on a road with no traffic. If he hadn't moved when I rode past, I wouldn't have noticed. He's a little survivor."

His crooked grin dissolved all the irritation she'd felt at being so rudely interrupted from a deserved rest.

"I'd planned to sneak him into the inn and give him a bath before anyone saw him," he continued. His expression was disarming. He looked like a boy caught snatching a piece of pie. It was more than a little disconcerting on a man who radiated self-confidence.

"Hopefully he'll make a full recovery," he added. "I want him to find a good home with kids and a family."

She waited as the dog hobbled awkwardly over the grass, this time stopping to hunch up and finish his chore.

"I like your Jeep," he said, seeming a little surprised at her transportation.

"I bought it from Josh. It's great for going up into the mountains."

He was about to say something but then Hobo limped over to Ross Taylor and waited to be lifted.

Her guest picked up Hobo with a tenderness that impressed her. She didn't want to be affected by it but, hells bells, she was.

She led the way to the front door and opened it.

"No key?" he asked without moving.

"We're not exactly a crime center," she said. "There hasn't been a robbery or break-in since I moved back here."

"How long ago was that?"

"A little more than five years ago, but I'm a native of Covenant Falls. My mother grew up here as did her mother and hers before that. Very little had changed in those years. Then Josh Manning appeared, then another veteran, and a third. Things started to change. In a good way."

"It's hard to imagine him as a builder and a businessman," her visitor said as he went through the door and she closed it behind him. "He was one of the toughest, no-nonsense staff sergeants in the army."

"He isn't much at explaining himself," she said with a smile. "He just likes to throw people into quicksand and see what happens."

"Are you one of those people?"

"I guess I am," Susan admitted.

"Does it work?"

"So far." *Until today.* She changed the subject. "You said the dog needs a bath. Isn't it going to be difficult with that leg?"

"Let's say I doubt if it's easy. But it has to be done. I suspect there's a few fleas along with dirt."

"I can wrap that leg in some plastic baggies and you can use the hand spray in the bathtub to wash him," she volunteered, surprising herself. But she knew how difficult it was to wash an uncooperative animal.

He raised an eyebrow.

Vagabond chose that moment to stride in from her favorite perch on the bookcase just below a window in the kitchen. She was not the most attractive cat in the neighborhood. She had her share of feral cat scars and was a wretched shade of orange. She purred a greeting until she saw the dog in Ross Taylor's arm. Her back went up and she hissed.

Susan couldn't blame the cat. She felt somewhat the same way about the intrusion. She was also struck by the similarity of names. Vagabond and Hobo. It was downright weird. It reflected similar thought patterns, and she didn't like that idea at all. She had nothing in common with this man, outside of the connection with Josh.

Vagabond retreated a few feet but not before expressing her irritation with an unholy squawk. Not a meow, but a high-pitched squawk.

"I don't think Hobo and I are welcome," her guest opined.

"She'll adjust. For a feral cat, she's turned into a diva," Susan said. "I never had a cat before. Always dogs when I was a kid. But Vagabond just showed up here one day and decided to stay. I didn't have much say in the matter."

"Then we have something in common," he said. "I didn't have much choice either, but this is a fleeting relationship. I hope to find him a home as soon as I see the veterinarian."

Their relationship would be fleeting, as well. They obviously didn't have much in common except falling victim to animals. He was overpowering, both physically and, well, personally. He dominated the space around him. And even with the fuzz on his face and being a sartorial disaster, he caused warning bells to ring in her. A small—very small—part of her might be just a little attracted to him, but she'd ignore that.

She counted the strikes against him. He rode a motorcycle. He was far too sure of himself. He was here temporarily. He was obviously a wanderer.

She felt she was inviting a tornado into her peaceful home.

"Sorry for ruining your night," he said with the first hint of concern. "I should have persisted in calling the inn."

"And then a very nice elderly couple would have had a dangerous drive home," she said.

"I just assumed there would be plenty of rooms."

"Don't apologize," she said. "The fault is mine. Not yours. The room *was* reserved for you." She paused, then added, "I'll show you upstairs and you can settle in while I gather up some extra towels."

She led the way up the stairs. The upstairs included two bedrooms and a bath. She'd turned the larger one into a guest room and the smaller one into a study/office/library. There was also a full bath in addition to the one downstairs that she usually used.

"This way," she said, and led him to the guest bedroom. She opened the door and waited while he entered and surveyed the room before placing the saddlebags on a chair.

"Nice," he said. "I think I'd better put Hobo in a bath before putting him down anywhere."

"Do you have dog shampoo?"

He looked blank for a moment. "I thought I could use human soap. The kind you find in hotels."

"You've never had a dog before?"

"When I was young. He was a ranch dog. He stayed outside and didn't get baths unless he ran into a skunk or something equally as noxious, then it was a hose.

I thought…hell, I guess I didn't think. I should have bought some along the way."

"A ranch dog? You've lived on a ranch?"

He hesitated, then replied, "It was a long time ago." His tone warned her off the subject.

She took the hint and said, "I use a liquid soap on my cat when she gets into something noxious. It's gentle and also helps with fleas. I'll bring a cup up with those towels. In the meantime, rub him around the ears and stomach to relax him."

"Thanks," he said with obvious relief. "I don't know if he's ever had a bath before. He sure as hell doesn't look like it."

"I have a laundry basket downstairs that will serve as a good bed for your dog."

"He's not my… "

"I know. That's what I kept telling Vagabond. She wasn't my cat, just an outside freeloader. Didn't do any good. An animal seems to pick their own person. Doesn't matter whether that person agrees or not. I certainly didn't. You just kinda get stuck and then, later, you're glad you got there."

His expression told her he had no intention of getting stuck.

She ignored it. "You think you can do it on your own?"

"Sure. It's just a bath," he said with male confidence.

She looked at the dog now nestled in his lap. "You two seem to be getting on rather well," she said.

He gave her a chagrined look, which softened the hard face. "We had a long ride together."

She tried not to let it affect her. "Take off your boots and socks and roll up those jeans. Prepare to get wet."

"Yes, ma'am," he said obediently but she saw a shadow of a smile cross his face as she turned and left.

Could this day get any worse?

Yeah, he reminded himself. It would have been, had the innkeeper not been so helpful. She was damned attractive, too. As weary as he was, he couldn't deny a certain spark flaring inside. It wasn't just her appearance that attracted him—the startlingly blue eyes, long dark hair, a body that was both athletic and womanly, and her easy smile—but her sense of humor and her ready acceptance of two strangers who must look like they'd stepped out of someone's nightmare.

Her smile was infectious and made him want to smile as well, even as he sat uncomfortably on the seat of a toilet in a decidedly feminine bathroom holding a wriggling, flea-infested mongrel at an ungodly hour and wondered what in the hell happened to his nice comfortable life. No complications. No responsibilities except to his current patients. That was his motto.

He silently condemned Josh for getting him into this mess. He'd just finished several assignments and had planned a biking trip up the California coast to Washington. No schedule except a few stops to see buddies. That was the way he liked it.

Hobo squirmed in his arms, but Ross hated to put him down on the rose-colored rug that covered a quarter of the pristine bathroom floor. He set the dog down in the empty tub instead and wondered again about his hostess as he awaited her return. Obviously she was dedicated to her job since she'd appeared in the middle of the night and opened her house to a stranger. Her smile was a killer.

Hobo tried to move again in an obvious effort to get more comfortable but he didn't make any noise. Not a whimper. "You're a good soldier," Ross said. "I wish you didn't need a bath but you're a mess right now. Not fit for polite company, and we're in polite company."

His years in the army had taught him to be observant, and he noticed details. The living area downstairs looked comfortable with large stuffed chairs, Western paintings and several full bookcases. There was a big flowering plant in front of the large window.

The guest bedroom looked equally as attractive with a queen-size bed covered by what looked like a hand-made quilt. Three large paintings of Western scenes decorated the walls. A comfortable-looking chair sat next to a window.

All the rooms had something in common. They were homey, comfortable and unpretentious.

He told himself none of it mattered. He was just here overnight and he was tired enough that the garage and a sleeping bag would have sufficed. He smothered a yawn. Damn but he was tired. He tried to snap back to the present.

He'd just finished taking off his boots and socks when she appeared with the bath supplies, along with a length of yarn.

She eyed his large naked feet and rolled up jeans. "Battle ready?" she asked.

"Can't be worse than serving under Josh," he said.

She laughed.

He liked the sound of it. In fact he liked a lot about her. He was impressed with her energy. He'd probably pulled her out of bed, then invaded her home with a filthy animal, not to mention his own sorry state, and she was being helpful. She'd been apologetic, businesslike and a tad defensive when he met her, and while he'd had little choice in accepting her offer, he hadn't been enthusiastic.

He still wasn't enthusiastic but he felt a hell of a lot better about the situation. He knew his size could be intimidating. She'd been a bit hesitant at first but then used her instincts. She was confident enough in her own abilities to bring him inside her home. He liked that.

Not, he reminded himself, that it mattered. He had no intention of staying in Covenant Falls one day longer than his two-week commitment to Josh. "I doubt he'll object any more than if it was the canine kind," he said of the shampoo.

She examined him. "It'll be easier to hold him while you sit on the edge of the tub with your feet in the water than leaning over the edge. If he's not familiar with a bath, he's going to fight you, but you'll be right there with him." She leaned over Hobo and covered the wounded leg with its splint with several plastic bags, then secured them with a piece of yarn.

"More comfortable than a rubber band," she said. "It may not be waterproof but it will help."

Makes sense. While still holding Hobo, Ross swung his long legs over the edge of the tub and perched on the narrow rim. It was…uncomfortable to say the least. Susan detached the hand showerhead from above and handed it to him. He turned the faucet on and water splashed all over him and the dog.

Hobo protested. He barked and tried to squirm out of Ross's grip. Ross held the dog with one hand as he frantically thrashed about, and gripped the showerhead in the other. His partner in dog torture leaned over and took the spray head from him and set it at a gentler output then handed it back to Ross. She'd taken off her shoes and sat on the rim of the tub with him and cooed over the dog as Ross rubbed a mixture of soap and water into the fur.

Hobo wasn't buying it. He kept wriggling. Ross was covered with water as Hobo tried to get out of his grasp, then shook water all over the bathroom and both of them.

Susan stood and stepped out of the tub, but Ross felt her eyes on him as he used more soap and water.

"Saints above," Susan exclaimed. "The dog is changing color." She gave him a sympathetic glance. "I think you're next when you're finished with Hobo," she said with what he considered a smirk.

He looked down at himself. He was soaked. His jeans were dirty from road dust and the rest of him was not much better. Why she ever let him in her house was beyond him. "I think you're right," he admitted.

"Is there anything else I can get you?" she said as she moved away from the bathroom.

"You're really not going to stay and help?"

"You're a big boy," she said, "with all four limbs intact. I think you can manage it."

Despite the frank words, he detected a hint of a smile in her eyes. She'd obviously enjoyed his discomfort.

"Maybe," he said. "But this seems beyond my expertise. I bow to yours."

"What is it they say about throwing a kid into the water to teach him to swim," she said, amusement tinting every word.

"They drown sometimes," he replied.

"I don't think you would be one of them," she shot back, then added, "I'm leaving at seven to help with checkout at the inn, but I'll have a thermos of coffee outside your room. There'll also be some pastries on the dining room table and orange juice in the fridge. Take your time," she added. "We probably won't have a room ready until ten."

"Thanks," he said.

"No need. I like dogs," she explained.

He noticed he wasn't included in the statement.

"Sleep in. And leave those clothes in the bathroom. I'll wash them and take them to the inn."

"Yes ma'am," he replied obediently.

"Just close the front door when you leave and make sure the cat doesn't go with you.

"And don't lock it," he recalled. "You must be the most trusting person in America."

"Nope." Her voice softened. "I just know Covenant Falls and I'm a fairly good judge of character after fifteen years in the hospitality field."

"Hobo and I thank you. You've gone way beyond the call of duty. I don't want to think what would have happened if I'd tried to wash Hobo by myself in a hotel room."

"Yes," she affirmed. "The bill would be staggering."

"Agreed," he replied. "I owe you."

"We aim to please," she said, then left him to finish on his own.

Ross smiled at the last comment even as the soapy dog tried again to get out of the tub and splashed a mixture of dirty, soapy water over his jeans.

He wanted Susan Hall back but damned if he was going to call for her. It must be near 2:00 a.m. now. He sure as hell wasn't going to admit he needed help in giving a small dog a bath. He recalled only too well the doubt in her eyes when he insisted he could do it on his own. Ha!

Finally, the exhausted little guy gave up and stayed relatively still. Ross finished rinsing the last of the soap and it was then he saw bite marks and other scars on the dog. He uttered a few "not for polite ears" oaths, and plucked Hobo from the deep tub only to be on the receiving side of another shower as the dog shook himself and more water landed on him and the floor.

Now he knew why Susan brought so many towels and why she'd escaped.

He dried Hobo as best he could. And then he saw more scars. A lot of old ones. Some not as old. He suddenly felt very protective. He would find Hobo a good home, one with children who would love him as he deserved to be loved.

Once reasonably clean, the dog was a tan and white mixture. The leg under the baggies was wet but not nearly as wet as the rest of him. He was, Ross had to admit, kinda engaging, if you liked little dogs. He liked big ones, especially when they belonged to someone else.

Ross used several of the towels to wipe the wet floor as Hobo huddled against the closed door, then neatly folded the wet towels and left them in the sink to drip.

There was one dry one left.

"Sorry, kiddo," he told Hobo. "You have to wait until I take my turn."

He rinsed out the tub, then hooked the showerhead back where it belonged.

He turned the temperature to hot, only to discover there was no hot left.

Resigned to another bump on this day, he took a cold shower, washing off two days on the road. He was freezing when he felt he'd made a dent. The rest had to wait until tomorrow. He definitely wasn't going to shave with cold water.

He left his wet clothes in the bathroom, and he and Hobo headed for the bedroom. He found a big, plastic clothes basket inside. It was lined with a thick, soft blanket. A dish of water was next to it along with a dish containing small pieces of chicken. For him there was a glass of milk and cookies on a bedside table.

Milk and cookies? He hadn't had that since he was a tyke.

Hobo had no reservations. He gobbled the chicken and drank a little water before Ross plucked him up and settled him in the basket. The dog did a couple of crooked circles on the soft material, then collapsed on it. He obviously didn't hold a grudge about the recent indignity and discomfort. But then *he* hadn't had a cold shower.

There was something backward about that.

Ross replaced his wet clothes with clean dry skivvies, then sat on the bed and ate the cookies and drank the milk.

Ross looked at the dog curled up and breathing easily, and his heart hitched a little. He decided he didn't begrudge the little guy all the hot water.

He turned off the light and sank into the bed. The crisp clean sheets felt great but his mind wouldn't shut off as fast as Hobo's apparently did.

His hostess's last smile—full of mischief and challenge—wouldn't leave his thoughts. It had been such a turnaround from the woman who'd walked into the inn with such businesslike determination. He certainly hadn't expected the invitation to her home, the ugliest cat he'd ever seen, her tenderness with Hobo nor her lack of concern as he and Hobo wrecked her bathroom.

And then cookies?

Watch it, Taylor.

It was a damn good thing he would be here a very short time before moving on. He would call Josh first thing in the morning and work out a schedule. The sooner he finished, the sooner he could take his long-anticipated drive up the coast.

Josh might be tamed, but he certainly never would be.

He turned over and closed his eyes, lulled by Hobo's soft, contented snoring.

Chapter 4

Streams of gold poured through the windows when Ross woke the next morning. Ross glanced at the clock on the table next to him. Nearly eight. It took him several seconds before he remembered where he was.

He rarely slept past six. His internal clock, in fact, usually woke him at 5:00 a.m. Then it all flooded back: the long ride, finding Hobo, arriving late in Covenant Falls only to find he had no room. Then, of course, the disastrous Hobo bath. He groaned. He didn't really want to think of that.

Ross glanced down at the basket. Hobo was curled up in a tight ball, his head resting on the bad leg.

Ross stood, stiff from the long ride yesterday. He did several quick stretches and felt better, then did some push-ups. He remembered something about coffee being outside his door. Hopefully, he went to get it. True to Ms.

Hall's word, a thermos sat on a tray, along with an oversize cup and several pastries. A note told him there was orange juice in the fridge.

Ross picked up the tray, took it inside and poured himself a cup of coffee.

Then he called Josh on his cell phone.

"Where in the hell are you?" Josh asked. "I knew you were delayed a day, but we expected you yesterday."

"You haven't talked to Susan Hall?"

"No. I checked with her around seven last night and she hadn't heard from you."

"I had a few delays and arrived a little after 11:00 p.m. I didn't want to disturb you."

"I *was* disturbed. I was worried."

"I didn't know you cared," Ross tossed back.

"I care about our schedule," Josh said grumpily. "I'll be right over to the inn. Ten minutes, say. We can have breakfast."

"Ah," Ross said, "I'm not exactly at the inn."

"Then where in the hell are you?"

Suddenly he realized he didn't want to say. Would it hurt Susan Hall's reputation? Or her job?

"I'll meet you at the inn in, say, thirty minutes," he suggested instead.

There was a pause, then Josh said, "I'll be there."

"I'll be bringing a friend."

"A friend?"

"You can meet when I arrive."

"She's not going to distract you?" Josh asked with new concern in his voice.

"It's not a she and when did you know me to be distracted?"

"I haven't seen you in several years."

"See you shortly," Ross said, and hung up before there were more questions. He took a deep swallow of coffee, which was, thankfully, strong and hot. He also ate the two pastries, drank a second cup of coffee and then went downstairs and had two large glasses of orange juice.

Bathroom was next. He'd been avoiding it and the mess. He'd cleaned it as well as he could last night but all the towels had been wet so he'd only hung his on the shower curtain rod. It was the best he could do.

To his amazement, it looked almost as clean and tidy as when he first saw it. How she managed that without waking him was a puzzlement. He took a quick hot shower, shaved for the first time in three days and dressed in the clean jeans and T-shirt in his saddlebags. Then he picked up Hobo and took him outside. He didn't have to worry about Hobo running away, not with his bad leg. He was pleasantly surprised when the dog promptly did his business in the yard. He was a smart little guy...

The two of them rode up to the inn four minutes later.

He plucked Hobo from the basket on his bike and entered the lobby. Hobo looked like a different dog from the one he'd picked up yesterday. He was still scrawny, and scars were still evident but at least he looked clean.

He headed toward the desk. Both Susan and a young man were working the desk, and she was busy with a young couple. She looked up at him. "He's in the library," she said, and turned back to the couple.

He stopped at the counter to pour a cup of coffee, then holding the coffee in one hand and Hobo in the other he walked to the library. Josh was tapping his fingers impatiently at the table Ross had used just a few hours earlier. A cup of coffee was on the table in front of him.

"Long time, no see," Ross remarked as he set Hobo on the floor.

"*This* is your friend?" Josh asked with a raised eyebrow.

"Not exactly a friend. I found him yesterday on a mountain road. He'd been shot and apparently left to die or someone thought he was already dead."

"So that's why you're late."

Ross nodded. "He was a mess. His leg looked infected and maybe broken and I did what I could but it wasn't much. I tried to find a veterinarian but the only one I located was closed. I had to stop frequently to check on him so I arrived around eleven last night, and the inn was full.

He took a sip of coffee, then continued. Since I hadn't arrived on Friday and it was late last night, Ms. Hall assumed I wouldn't show last night either and gave the room to an elderly couple. In lieu of a room here, she suggested I stay at her house overnight. She said she'd rented out a room before. And apparently I looked harmless. And desperate."

"You? Harmless. Ha!" Josh said. "It's a good thing she didn't call me. I seem to remember something else."

"Well, not to worry. I spent the night giving Hobo a bath and getting one from him, as well. I don't think he'd ever had one before. You should have seen him…"

"You and that little dog?" A smile was spreading over Josh's face.

"Don't get the wrong idea. I'm going to turn him over to the veterinarian today. I hear she's in the dog rescue business."

"Not going to happen," Josh said. "She has more rescue dogs than she can handle right now." He paused. "You really spent the night at Susan's?"

"Yeah. Susan didn't mention it this morning?"

"Nope. She was busy when I came in. She runs the inn completely free of me and Nate, my partner. Does all the marketing, and she's great with guests, but she doesn't usually take in guests at her home."

"I think Hobo and I looked pitiful."

"Pitiful? You?" Josh replied.

"Hell, I had three days of beard and two days of dirt on me. I looked pretty deplorable, and Hobo here looked even worse. He had a lifetime of dirt on him. It all went well until we got to the bath…"

Josh raised an eyebrow.

"It was all very proper. She abandoned me when Hobo decided he didn't want a bath."

"Abandoned?"

Ross chuckled. "You're just full of questions," he said. "Well, she provided soap and water and left me to cope. I suppose she thought it was a battle between two males. The bathroom was a lake before I finished."

Josh grinned. "That little dog? I thought better of you."

"So did I. What's a little bath? I thought. After all, I rescued him and deserved some respect. Unfortunately he had none."

"I like him already," Josh said.

"He's a fine dog," Ross said, trying to contain the hope in his voice. "Just needs a good home. Don't you want a dog?"

"I'll tell you what," Josh replied. "Because—and only because—you're my friend I'll consider…"

"Taking him?" Ross said hopefully.

"Hell, no, but I'll teach you how to cope with a pet. Eight animals came along with my wife and her son."

"Eight?" Ross couldn't keep the horror from his voice.

"Yeah. Five dogs, a crazy cat and two horses. Six dogs if you include Amos." Not only did I gain a wife and son, but a damn zoo.

"Then you wouldn't even notice one more," Ross countered.

"My wife might not, but I would," Josh replied. "Just wait until you meet her. I was the ogre of Covenant Falls until she rudely interrupted my self-imposed seclusion. She's a people whisperer as well as an animal whisperer."

"How is Amos? I'd heard you found him and adopted him."

"How did you hear that?"

"The outfit's grapevine," Ross explained. "Your search for your partner's military dog has become legend. I was real sorry to hear about Dave."

"That's how I came to be here," Josh replied. "You probably heard he died saving my life. Well, he had no family and left me a cabin here. I was riddled with guilt and didn't want the damn thing. But then I found Amos who had canine PTSD and we had to go somewhere. The cabin was in pretty bad condition. I thought I would fix it up, sell it and Amos and I would go be hermits somewhere. Eve, the mayor, and had other ideas.

"After a rocky start, Amos is fine now. He's at home now, taking care of the rest of the brood. He'll be at the party tonight." Josh unwound his long legs. "You'd better get your key, then I'll take you to Jubal's ranch and you can meet him and look around.

"You said he was a former SEAL?"

"Yeah. Jubal had a rough time as a prisoner of a terrorist group. The physical damage kept him from returning to the SEALs. He came here to see an army buddy and fell in love with a horse. Riding helped him so much he wanted to share the experience. Thus, the New Beginnings Ranch. Right now, it's a work in progress, which is why I wanted you here. A two- or four- or six-week stay doesn't help much if our veterans go home and fall back into depression. We're hoping you can help them establish habits they'll take home with them."

"It's at Jubal's ranch?" Ross asked.

Josh nodded. "Jubal's neighbor—Luke—is a Vietnam vet. He's nearly seventy but could probably beat the hell out of me. Both he and his wife have been raising horses and teaching horsemanship for years. Although the bunkhouse and stables for New Beginnings are on Jubal's property, we're using Luke's land and cattle, as well. Some other ranchers are participating as well by loaning us horses and equipment. This has turned into a community project."

He took a sip of coffee. "There's a cookout tonight at New Beginnings and everyone involved will be there, including the program's participants. In fact, they're in charge of the menu."

Ross nodded, trying not to show his reluctance. He hadn't been on a ranch since he was ten years old. Even the smell of hay brought back flashbacks he'd spent his life trying to forget. Only Josh could have lured him back. He was the one man that Ross couldn't refuse.

"I'll pick up my room key and leave my stuff there," he said. "I'm not sure what to do with the little guy here."

"Bring him along," Josh said. "You can ride with me. Jubal's ranch is just a few miles out of town."

"Give me ten minutes, tops. " He stood and went into the lobby to the main desk. Susan was checking another couple out, and Mark was helping someone else. No one else was in line.

She finished with the departing couple, and Ross approached the desk.

Susan smiled. "You survived the bath. I knew you had it in you," she said lightly, laughter dancing in her eyes.

"Then you were more optimistic than me," he replied, charmed by her smile. "Thanks for breakfast and for cleaning the bathroom. And I have to admit the bed was far superior to your garage floor."

"You're welcome. I hope you'll like the room here, as well." She'd suddenly turned back into the efficient innkeeper. Her dark hair was in a neat French twist, and she wore business garb: blue slacks, white blouse and blue jacket. More interesting was that nonstop energy despite little sleep.

If she noticed his scrutiny she didn't show it as she typed away on the computer. "You got lucky," she said. "One of the first guests to check out had the room I had in mind for you. Number 18. It's been cleaned. Just turn left and go down the hall. It's on the right at the end of the corridor.

"There's an outside door next to the room," she continued in a businesslike tone. "You can park there, and there's a green area for Hobo. He's the only dog in residence now. He's certainly the cleanest."

"I apologize for the bathroom," he said. "I did my best to clean it."

"I've seen worse," she teased.

"When?"

"When I bathed Vagabond the first time. And the second time when she got into something nasty. And, unfortunately, the third." Then she changed subjects. "I'll have your clothes ready later."

"You don't have to do that."

"No problem. They're in the machine at home. It's the least I could do after giving your room away. I'll leave them in your room later." She handed him a paper. "Just sign here with your name, address and contact number. I won't need a credit card since Mr. Morgan is taking care of everything."

After he completed registration, she handed him an actual metal key and briefly explained the amenities. "Starting at 6:00 a.m., there's coffee and pastries here in the lobby. There's complimentary wine in the afternoon in the library. The dining room isn't open except on weekends, but two restaurants—Maude's and the Rusty Nail—deliver. There's menus in the room." Her tone was neutral.

He was just another guest now.

"How's Hobo?" she asked.

"Clean, thanks to you. He collapsed in the basket last night. The bath wore him out. And me."

She smiled at that. "I hope you enjoy your stay," she said as she turned to an older man who had just approached the desk.

To his surprise, the dismissal stung. On the other hand, it was probably a good thing. He was only going to be here a short time and he expected Josh would keep him busy. After that, he wasn't sure. Could be more jobs in Hollywood. He often stayed in private homes or the client paid for an expensive hotel room. The pay was lucrative and allowed him to do pro bono work, mainly with VA facilities.

The experiences were mixed, but he must be doing

something right because he continued to have referrals. Problem was expectations. The client—they usually preferred that description to patient—often had unrealistic goals. They tended to return to the set before they were ready. He left the desk and reported back to Josh. "The room is ready," he said. "Give me five minutes to leave my stuff there. Since you've had so much experience with dogs, you can look after Hobo until I get back."

He plopped Hobo in Josh's lap and left before he or the dog could protest. He checked out the room, then went to his bike and drove it around a narrow path to the side of the building and parked it. He threw the saddlebags over his shoulder and unstrapped the two baskets on the back of the bike, then took them inside to his temporary home.

Like Susan's house, the room was warm and welcoming. Quilts rather than comforters topped the beds. The walls were decorated with prints of mountains, just as her home had been. The interior sign with standard fire and theft precautions included a drawing of two camels looking at the occupants with suspicion.

It made him smile.

He wondered if Susan Hall had named the inn. It sounded like her often-whimsical sense of humor.

Josh was waiting. Ross locked the door and went to meet his friend.

Hobo was sitting in Josh's lap, looking at him with adoration. He hadn't done that with Ross, but then Josh hadn't dragged him across country in a small basket. Still, he felt aggrieved at the lack of loyalty.

"We should get going," Josh said. "Jubal is waiting for us."

"What about Hobo?" he asked.

"Have you fed him?" Josh asked.

"Your innkeeper was kind enough to leave some corn flakes for him this morning. I'll have to find some dog food until I can find him a home. And I do want that leg looked at. Do you know when the vet will be back?"

"I called while you were in the room. She hopes to be back late this afternoon. They've narrowed the search area. She'll call as soon as she arrives, but he looks good aside from being thin and that leg. I supposed you designed that little splint."

He nodded. "I don't think he needs it, though. I've watched him put some weight on it."

Josh's cell phone rang. He looked at the number. "I should get this."

"Go ahead," Ross said.

He heard Josh's quick questions. "When? Where is he? Are you all right?"

Then he hung up. "Sorry, I have to leave. My stepson fell while chasing one of our dogs. My wife thinks he broke his arm."

"Go," Ross insisted. "I can find my way to the ranch."

"Wait here," Josh said. He disappeared from the library and returned almost immediately.

"Susan will take you," he said. "She knows as much about this program as I do." He left before Ross could protest.

If he wanted to.

He discovered he didn't. Josh's last sentence intrigued him. *She knows as much about this program as I do.* Yet another side to the innkeeper?

Twenty minutes later, Ross sat next to Susan in her Jeep. Because his long legs filled the space on the floor, Hobo sat on his lap.

"You're involved in the equine program as well as the inn?" he asked. He wanted to discover more about his driver.

"I'm just a volunteer," she replied.

Watch it. He kept telling himself that. He'd been interested last night. He liked her. He was attracted to her although she wasn't the type of woman who usually drew his interest. Maybe because he usually looked for someone who, like him, wasn't interested in a long relationship.

Susan, on the other hand, was a nester. It was obvious from her home. It shouted permanence while he was a bone deep wanderer.

It was clear she loved her job, her home and the town and he wasn't surprised she was involved with Josh's program. He'd noticed how deftly she interacted with guests at the inn, including him.

It was a rare talent but then she seemed to be a woman of many talents. She was as comfortable bathing a filthy dog as she was in business clothes talking to customers. She seemed equally at ease with both her boss and her employees.

What he couldn't figure out was why a woman so attractive was apparently single.

Not that his impressions mattered. He liked his life now. He'd worked hard for it. After years in the army and more years getting his degree, he relished the freedom to go where he wanted when he wanted. He enjoyed working with people, helping them mend and then going on his way.

"Are you still with me?" Her words broke into his thoughts.

She was also a mind reader. "Yeah," he said. "It's fine country. Good grass."

"You sound like you're familiar with it."

"Not really. It's just obvious." He hoped the tone in his voice would quiet the questions. His fingers kneaded Hobo's fur but he gentled them as soon as he realized he might be too rough. Those damned emotions were kicking up.

"This is New Beginnings Ranch," Susan said as she turned onto a gravel road lined on both sides with white fences. Horses grazed in the pasture and several looked up as Susan turned toward a group of buildings fronted by an unassuming one-story brick home.

Memories started flooding him. He tensed as they approached what appeared to be a stable about forty yards from the house. *You're not a kid anymore. Stay in the present. Don't go back now.*

"Tell me about the owner," Ross said. Josh had said a little, but Ross wanted to know more if he was working with him.

"Ex-Navy SEAL Jubal Pierce. You probably heard about him when he appeared after two years of captivity in Africa. His body had been starved, and there was muscle and bone damage. He didn't have the strength to return to the SEALS and was at loose ends. The police chief here, another vet, was a friend and invited him to stay in Covenant Falls for a few days.

"Obviously he stayed."

Susan nodded. "He's not hesitant to admit he was a mess when he came here. His captivity and the loss of his team really affected him. He couldn't understand why he survived when the others didn't. He was running down the road we just traveled when he stopped to watch horses in the pasture. One reminded him of a horse his father once owned. He met Luke, the owner of the ranch, who invited him to ride that horse. The two became good friends, then partners. That's how it started."

It sounded familiar, too familiar. He didn't know whether she was aware of the sudden tightening of his body.

She continued, "He started riding here and fell in love with both the horse and our local doctor. In that order. He believes riding literally saved him, thus the name, New Beginnings Ranch."

"And your part?"

"Very small. I'm helping with publicity and coordination with the VA who refers vets to us. Neither Josh nor Jubal have the patience or tact to do it. I double majored in hospitality and marketing in college and, believe me, you learn tact in both fields. I also try to locate sponsors and generally help where I can."

Ross mentally scolded himself. He'd been grateful last night to a woman who worked at the inn. Her smile revived something inside him. Now, though, she was apparently much more than an inn employee. Not that it mattered. He just should have recognized it sooner.

"Do you ride?" he asked.

"Since I was a kid. Practically everyone in Covenant Falls does. That's why the entire town is behind this. There's another reason. Even before the recent arrival of vets, a large percentage of our population are veterans or have a son or daughter in the military." She paused. "What about you? Do you ride now?"

He hesitated, then admitted, "Not since I was a kid."

The conversation ended as she drove into a parking area and stopped. She stepped out of the Jeep and Ross followed, trying to puzzle the relationships in the town.

When Josh called him, he had no idea of the scope of what they were trying to do.

Josh had sent him information on the different veterans in Covenant Falls and their roles with the program. He hadn't mentioned Susan.

Before they reached the door, a tall lean man in jeans and a plaid shirt emerged from the house and met them. He thrust out his hand to Ross. "I'm Jubal Pierce. Good to have you here. Josh says good things about you. Said you were a damn good medic. Now a damn good physical therapist." Ross had no idea how Josh would know the latter. But then Josh had always been prepared in whatever he did.

He didn't know how to reply so he just let the comment go. He released the strong grip.

"I take it Susan has taken good care of you," Jubal said.

"She has." Ross didn't elaborate.

"Good. I'll give you a brief tour and introduce you to our current gang of vets." He turned to Susan. "And what do you have in your arms?"

"This is Hobo," Susan said. "Ross acquired him on the way here. He's hoping he can foist Hobo on you or one of your vets for a few hours if not forever."

"He does, huh?" Jubal said with the hint of a smile. "Why don't you take him to the stables?" he asked Susan. "There's several guys looking after their horses back there. One of them will look after him for an hour or so while I talk to Ross and show him around."

"Me?" Susan asked.

"They'll do anything *you* ask."

"Why do I think you're conning me again?"

"Because you know me too well," Jubal said. "And also because it's true."

"Well, I like them, too," she said. "I'll find a temporary caretaker for Hobo, then head back to the inn. I've left the inn on Mark's young shoulders. I'll be back for the cookout."

"Why don't you come earlier? We're going to put some of the vets who have some riding experience on horses after lunch. Why don't you ride with us? Kate's going and she might want female company."

"I would like that." Susan said.

"By the way, our guys really enjoyed the pageant last night. It was a great idea to invite them. I never would have thought of it. They got to know each other and had something to talk about other than themselves. It also got them excited about the area."

She nodded. "What about Kate? Is she comfortable with the rest being all guys?"

"She seems to be. She lived in the field with men during the years she was in Iraq and Afghanistan. She's not going to take any crap from them. Luke says she did some riding years ago and doesn't need much instruction. Still, you might spend some time with her if you can manage it."

"I can do that," Susan said. "There's only a few guests remaining at the inn, and Mark can take care of them. He's really appreciative of the extra hours, especially when there's not much to do. He can study while making money." And with that, she picked up the dog and left.

Chapter 5

Ross turned to Jubal as Susan walked swiftly toward what was obviously the stable. "Does she ever slow down?" he asked.

"Not that I've noticed. Josh calls her Wonder Woman. Nearly every veteran who comes here falls in love with her, regardless of their age. All she offers is friendship but that's still a gift."

"I take it that's a warning, but it's not necessary," Ross said. "I avoid mixing pleasure with business. I like her. In fact, I'm in awe of her, but that is as far as it goes."

Jubal just raised an eyebrow, then said, "Speaking of irresistible women, come and meet my wife. She's been looking forward to meeting you."

Once they were inside a comfortable living room, a tall fine-looking woman entered the room. Jubal put an arm around her. "Ross, meet Lisa. She's a doctor and the brains behind the program. Also cook and bottle washer. She's been in the kitchen making a giant salad for the cookout tonight. The vets are doing the rest."

Ross nodded. Lisa Pierce was an attractive woman with expressive dark brown eyes. The former SEAL had married well. Lisa gave him a blinding smile. "I'm delighted to meet you. You're the glue we need to get this thing going."

"Glue?"

"We have horses. We have good trainers and riding instructors. One of them is a national champion women's barrel racer. Now that we're open, we're getting interest from the VA and some sponsors. What we don't have is a physical therapist to help us with the conditioning and tell us what *not* to do."

"I'm just here temporarily," Ross replied but softened it with a wry smile. "I think it's great what you're doing here," he added, although he was beginning to think Covenant Falls was a Venus flytrap for veterans.

"Gotcha," Jubal said, but Ross thought he saw a gleam in his eyes. He was having none of it. Two weeks max. Not one day longer.

Lisa left them and during the next hour, Jubal talked about the program and where he wanted to take it.

"Luke's more like a father than a partner. He's in his seventies but he has more energy than someone half his age. Between the two of us," he continued, "we have twenty-five trained riding horses. Eighteen are designated for the veteran program. The others are for our personal use or, in Luke's case, breeding. We started with twelve vets, grew to fourteen today. We want to go to sixteen, including the physically impaired. The program is six weeks long, the last week being a weeklong trail trip into the mountains."

Ross found himself impressed with what the former SEAL had accomplished in the twelve months since they'd started planning New Beginnings.

"The program is based on research prepared by Travis Hammond, former army major and another army friend of Josh's," Jubal said. "He's a high school coach here now and helps out when he can." Jubal picked up a thick notebook and handed it to Ross. "He visited a number of existing programs and gave us options. It's all in there."

Ross looked at the book dubiously. "No electronic format?"

"We have an official version online but the notebook includes personal handwritten notes about individuals," he said. "A lot of it is private, and to tell you the truth we don't have the electronic expertise to ensure the privacy of individuals. This will give you more of a feel for what Travis thought about the programs he saw and the people he met. His wife's comments are in there, as well. She's a reporter and a big fan of the program. I think you'll find their comments interesting."

Ross took it, saw the name and blinked. "Travis Hammond? I know him. Has Josh recruited the whole damn unit to help?"

"Just a few of the best," Jubal replied. "I'm about the only outsider. And maybe Danny. He's a young amputee who came here with Travis. It's amazing how riding has helped him gain confidence. He could get a job at any ranch now. If you need anything, and I'm not here, go to him."

"That's another goal of ours," he continued. "We want to create new job possibilities for these guys. After six weeks, they'll be good horsemen. They will be living, thinking and dreaming horses. That was one of Travis's recommendations. Create new job avenues as well as re-build confidence and comradery." It's the beginning of the football season and he's swamped, but he's going to try to be here tonight. You can ask him questions then.

"The big question," Jubal continued, "is whether we now need a full-time physical therapist or whether you can help develop a physical therapy program that will work for most of the veterans in the future, one they can take home with them."

"I like what you're doing," Ross said. "Just off the top of my head, at a minimum I think you should have a physical therapist on hand with each new group to as-sess their PT needs and develop a plan for each one. Be better if he—or she—can return midterm or even more often to reassess their progress."

Ross hesitated, then continued, "It would be prefer-able, of course, to have a full-time therapist if the money is available, but I don't think it's essential unless you ac-cept severely physically impaired individuals." Another pause, then he added, "I assume you have psychologists involved."

"Two," Jubal said. "One is an army psychologist in Texas. He helped develop the program and recruited a local doc from Pueblo to hold weekly sessions with the guys and be available when necessary."

Jubal walked over to the window and stared out at the riding ring. "I was a mess when I came here. Josh prob-ably told you some of the story. My body was a wreck after two years of near starvation and chained to a side of a hut or a tree. Not to mention periodic beatings. I no longer qualified physically for the SEALs. I was in a downhill spiral. No place to go. Nowhere to belong. Luke and this town probably saved my life. It did the same for Josh.

My greatest fear now," he continued, "is moving too fast and causing harm. We need someone to say 'whoa, you're moving too fast, or you need more professional help or you're missing a component.'" He shrugged his shoulders. "We're all military. We sometimes expect more than we should."

"I'll do what I can in the next two weeks," Ross said, and changed the subject. "What about Susan? What part does she play in this?"

"Organizer. Promoter. She works with the Veterans Administration to identify potential participants. And that's just the beginning. Give her an idea and she'll run with it." He raised an eyebrow. "Interested?"

"Just…curious. Her study was full of books of every type, including a lot of travel books. Made me wonder why she stays in a small town."

"Her study?" The question came quick.

Ross hurried to explain. "There were no available rooms at the inn when I arrived last night. She offered a room in her house. I might add that Vagabond disapproved, especially when I brought a dog with me.

"Vagabond disapproves of everyone," Jubal said.

"I take it the entire town feels protective," he added, "although I doubt she needs it. She warned me that she knew Karate."

Jubal chuckled. You have that right. She is one of the town's favorite people and like a sister to most of us vets. Her personal goal is to grow a town where young people can stay and thrive. Until recently there were few opportunities. Now it's growing, mainly because of her and Andy, a former army surgical nurse who heads our Chamber of Commerce."

Ross nodded. "As to the program, I'll do what I can."

"I admit to hoping you could stay beyond two weeks. You can ride our horses. Explore this area a little. It's really breathtaking, particularly our falls."

"Tempting, but I've been planning a bike trip up the coast for years. I've had to postpone it twice. I promised myself I won't do it again."

"We'll take what we can get," Jubal said. "Let's go out to the stables. You can meet some of the vets. Maybe take a ride with a group we're taking out in an hour."

"I don't ride," Ross said.

"Have you ever?"

"When I was very young," Ross admitted reluctantly. "I doubt anything stuck."

"Strangely enough, it does," Jubal said. "I felt the same. Hadn't been on a horse since I was seven. Then I sat on Jacko, my horse now, and something clicked. Riding is something you never really forget." He added, "You'll understand the program better if you do."

Ross wanted to say no. Too many bad associations. But hell, they were asking these vets to overcome their demons and apparently riding helped Jubal. Maybe it was time for him to slay some of his memories. "I'll give it a try."

Jubal grinned. "Great. I know the perfect horse for you. His name is Cajun. He's a great riding horse but he's bigger than the others, which is probably why he wasn't selected by one of the vets. They get to choose the horse that will stay with them throughout the program.

Ross nodded reluctantly. There was no way he could

connect with the guys without sharing some of their experiences, including, he suspected, the aches and pain.

Jubal held out his hand. "Welcome to the gang."

After delivering Ross to Jubal, Susan headed toward the stables with Hobo in her arms. She didn't worry about his running away. A tortoise could outrun him with his injury. But she didn't know what his reaction would be to the horses and new people.

After finding a temporary caretaker for Hobo, she wanted to check on the inn and change into riding clothes now that she was invited to ride with Jubal and a group of the vets. Her to-do list also included a stop at the drugstore—the only store open on Sunday—to pick up a collar and leash for Hobo. She suspected Jubal would keep Ross busy all morning.

She reached the stable, which was fairly quiet this time of day. Today was the first day of actual instruction for this new wave of vets. Yesterday had been spent choosing horses and getting to know them. Grooming had been the first lesson. Grooming and just visiting with their horse.

She'd escaped the inn long enough yesterday to watch the horse selection process. The available horses were gathered in the outdoor riding ring, and each veteran walked among them until magic happened and he or she just seemed to pick each other out. She'd noticed—or someone noticed for her—that shy individuals usually selected shy horses and outgoing ones would select a more active horse.

More than half of the participating vets had little—if any—experience with horses and were apprehensive at first. Once they selected a horse, or a horse picked them, the rider and horse would stay together throughout the length of the program, each day strengthening that first tentative bond. It was *their* horse and it was the *best* horse. Each was determined to prove it.

From the moment of selection, the veteran was responsible for feeding, watering, exercising and grooming their horse as long as they stayed. After leaving the program, they were welcome to return to ride the horse, or just visit. Susan thoroughly enjoyed watching the bonds with and pride in their animal grow as each vet first mounted a horse, then learned over the weeks to trot, canter and gallop. Even herd cattle.

But today she had other things to do and, first, was to find a temporary caretaker for Hobo. She saw Scott Wilson, who was feeding his chosen horse a carrot. She'd met Scott when he'd visited the ranch and applied for the program. He'd stayed at the inn that weekend.

He turned toward her when she approached with Hobo. "Whatcha got there, Ms. Hall?"

"It's Susan, Scott. I don't answer to 'Ms.'"

He grinned. "You just did."

"So I did, but that doesn't mean I'll do it the next time," she said. "Do you have an hour or so free?"

"Sure do. I've groomed, watered and fed Brandy. "My lesson isn't until two. I'm just hanging with my girl, here," he said as he cast a look at a bay horse.

"Could you look after this little guy for about an hour? He belongs to the new physical therapist, who is talking to Jubal. I have some errands to run."

"Sure. I like dogs. I'll take care of him like he was my own," Scott said.

"How did you like the pageant last night?" she asked. All the incoming vets had been invited. Most accepted.

"Liked it a lot," Scott replied. "Tell you the truth, I didn't want to go. I heard there would be a large audience and I'm...not comfortable with loud noises, but I was fine with the other guys there."

"That's terrific. Maybe next year you can be in it."

"No. I don't..."

"I heard you have a good voice. Maybe you'll sing something tonight at the cookout."

"I... I don't know..."

"You don't have to," she said. "It's up to you." Susan handed the dog over to Scott. "Thanks for looking after Hobo. He's had a hard time."

"I sure will, Ms.... I mean Susan."

Pleased she had broken through his shyness, she hurried out. She could have taken Hobo with her, but she knew how important it was for the vets to take responsibility.

When she arrived at the inn, Mark was back in a chair behind the desk working on the computer. He'd always worked extra hours on Sunday so Judy could go to church with her family.

He was happy to do it since he could study when it was slow.

"All is peaceful," he said. "Mr. and Mrs. Murray and their friends have decided to stay another day, but they're out for the day. They decided to do the Jeep trip to the gold mines."

"Great. Horace will be a happy man. That's three trips this week. He loves putting on the old-time miner persona."

"Oh, and we've had several new reservations, including the couple you helped last night. They want to come back and do some exploring. They're also thinking about holding a family reunion here."

"Wow," Susan replied. "That paid off." The reservation more than made up for giving away Ross's room.

"How does the new group of vets look?" Mark asked.

"Raring to go today, but I wouldn't want their aches and pains tomorrow."

He grinned. "I already sympathize."

She loved that the entire town had taken an interest in New Beginnings. Everyone wanted to help. Maude, who owned the most popular restaurant in town, had promised freshly baked rolls and cakes for tonight's cookout. Ranchers donated meat. Farmers sent veggies.

"Thanks for filling in today," she said.

"It's quiet and I can study. I expect it will stay that way all day."

When she arrived home, Vagabond complained bitterly about being abandoned. Susan tried to soothe her by running her hands through the cat's thick fur. Didn't work. Several pieces of chicken did. All was forgiven.

A coffee cup and one dish had been rinsed and placed in the sink. That and Ross's jeans and shirt in the dryer were the only reminders of her unexpected visitor last night. She grinned as she recalled the frustrated look on his face amidst the flood in the bathroom. She took his clothes from the dryer and folded them.

She changed from her business clothes into a shirt, jeans and riding boots. Although her family had never owned a horse, this was ranch country and she'd been riding since she was eight. Luke, in fact, had taught her to ride.

She used a touch of lipstick and worked her hair into

one long braid as she usually did when riding. She stared at herself in the mirror and tried to see herself as others did. Ordinary dark brown hair. Ordinary blue eyes. Medium height. Medium build. Nothing outstanding or memorable. For a tenth of a second she wondered what type Ross liked; then she pushed the thought back in a box where it belonged. She didn't care. It was nothing to her.

She had friends, a job she loved, a life that suited her. She'd tried the love thing, and it hadn't been satisfactory. In truth, it had been a nightmare, and she had no intention of stepping into another one. She'd fought too hard to gain control over her own life.

She refilled Vagabond's food and water bowls. "Sorry, kiddo," she said. "Gotta go, but I promise, no visitors tonight."

She grabbed Ross's now-clean clothes, then headed to the town drugstore. She would just make it back for the afternoon ride with several of the vets who'd had some riding experience. She wondered whether Ross would ride along, as well.

Or did he not ride anything other than his humongous motorcycle? She didn't know much about him. She knew he liked dogs, or at least couldn't leave an injured one. She knew he rode a motorcycle, but not whether he had a car in addition to the bike. She knew he didn't have a permanent home. On a sudden whim, she used her cell phone to search Ross Taylor, physical therapist.

To her dismay there were a large number of Ross Taylors who were physical therapists. She started running through the list, discarding this one and that one. She visited several websites without success. She finally found a mention of *her* Ross Taylor through an article with a photo.

She scanned the article. The headline was titled Physical Therapist to the Stars.

Huh!

She knew it was *her* Ross Taylor by the photo. It was not posed. He was obviously caught by surprise while exiting the home of a popular action film star.

The article mentioned that he wouldn't talk to reporters but that he apparently had worked with several action stars and stuntmen who'd been injured in films and needed a quick return. The actor's agent later identified him. The obviously frustrated reporter added in the story that he couldn't be reached for comment.

She read the article again and did some more searching. Nothing. No website, no other social media. He apparently avoided attention like the plague. There was no question in her mind that those stars paid a lot of money to a physical therapist who didn't talk to reporters.

One thing was for sure, he wouldn't be staying long. No wonder he carried so few belongings with him. He could buy new ones wherever he went. It was interesting, she also noted, that Josh hadn't given her more details. But then Josh had always been a man of few words. He probably figured it was none of anyone's business.

And, she told herself, it certainly wasn't hers.

But it definitely added another side to Ross Taylor and made it even more apparent that she should avoid him like the plague. His lifestyle was definitely not hers. His patients were wealthy actors rather than those who needed help for everyday living. In Las Vegas, she'd been exposed to stars and glamour and the excess that often went with it. Never again.

Yes, she really did need to avoid him. The problem was Covenant Falls. It was too small not to bump into the same people every day. Not only that, he was staying in her inn and working in a place that meant so much to her.

Horse feathers! The old cowboy expression was all she could come up with to express her frustration. She refilled Vagabond's water and food dishes and hurried out.

After finishing their meeting, which took all morning, Jubal made them both some sandwiches before walking over to the stable area. The smell of smoking meat came from behind the long building Ross now knew was the bunkhouse. Several men were riding horses in the ring as an older woman gave instructions. "That's Luke's wife," Ross explained. "She's a great instructor. This is first time in the saddle for this group of riders."

To the left, another group of vets stood next to saddled horses.

Jubal steered him over to them. "This is the group going out now. They all have some previous riding experience," Jubal said. "Luke and I are taking them on a trail ride to determine how much."

He introduced Ross to Luke, a tall lean man with thick white hair and a slow smile. Luke shook his hand. "Good to meet you," he said. "You were the missing piece."

Jubal turned to the others and introduced them to Ross. "Sorry I'm late," Jubal said to the group of veterans. "This is Ross Taylor, physical therapist, friend of Josh's and ex-Ranger medic. He'll be joining us for the next two weeks and you'll all have sessions with him. He'll work you hard, but he's a good man to have around."

As Jubal introduced them, Ross shook the hand of each of the budding riders, including the woman. Kate was thin. Her eyes looked hollow. But she summoned up a half smile.

"I'm taking Ross to the stables," Jubal told the riders. "You go on. We'll catch up with you.

Having no logical excuse to delay, Ross walked with Jubal into the stables. It was the moment Ross dreaded. The scent of hay stirred memories he'd tried to suppress: the body swinging from a rope attached to a support beam in the barn, the anxious whinnying of horses that sensed something was wrong. It was the night his childhood ended. That night—and the aftermath—haunted him for years and became even more real when he entered a barn or stable.

He'd had flashbacks from his army days as well, particularly when there was a sudden bright light or the sound of loud thunder that could have been rocket fire, but *they* didn't bring back the horror of that barn.

He clenched his fists and followed Jubal into the barn, willing himself to ignore the images that swept through him as he walked past a line of stalls. He'd feared it would happen when he accepted Jubal's offer, but he hadn't been able to refuse. He knew the hell of PTSD, the inability to fit back into a civilian community that didn't, couldn't, begin to understand PTSD or the loss of a close band of comrades who shared years of life and death experiences.

But damn, maybe it was time to face some of those demons as Josh and the others were asking these veterans to do.

"Anything wrong?" Jubal's voice broke through the flashback.

Had he been that transparent? "No," he lied.

Ross was grateful Jubal didn't ask more questions.

Instead, Jubal led the way into the tack room. Twenty or so saddles sat on racks along the walls. Bridles hung above them.

Hobo barked from where he sat beside a young man who was polishing a saddle, then limped over to Ross while making little crying noises.

"You must be Mr. Taylor," the young man said as he stood. "I'm Danny. I took over this little guy for you."

Ross nodded. "Make it Ross," he said. "How has Hobo been doing?"

"I think he's been looking for you," Danny said. "Every time someone comes in, he stands and looks, then his head droops and he sits again, never taking his eyes from the door."

Probably thought he had been abandoned again. Ross knew that feeling.

He picked Hobo up and rubbed his ears. The darn dog was getting to him. He hadn't had a dog since that last night in the family barn. He'd learned in succeeding years not to get attached to people or animals.

Jubal apparently didn't notice his distraction or, if he did, chose not to mention it. "Hi, Danny," he said, then turned back to Ross. "I told you about him. He's on staff. He's worked here since the beginning. If you need anything, ask him. He knows all the horses, all the volunteers and where everything is. He even helped build the bunkhouse."

"Thanks for taking care of this guy," Ross said while rubbing Hobo's ears.

"He's a good dog," Danny said.

"Can you keep him a bit longer?" Jubal asked Danny. "I want to show Ross the stable."

"Sure," the young man said. "Hobo and I are friends."

Ross handed Hobo back to the young man. He followed Jubal through the door to the stall area and down the aisle past several horses until they reached the next to last one. A handsome buckskin stuck his head out and nuzzled Jubal.

"This is Jacko," Jubal said. "I wanted you to meet him. He's responsible for all this. When I stopped in Covenant Falls to see a friend, I was in a bad way. While running one day, I saw some horses grazing and stopped at the fence to watch. Jacko came over to the fence and we were instant buddies. Luke appeared and we started talking. He asked if I wanted to ride Jacko. When I got onto the saddle, I felt at peace with myself for the first time in years. I started to feel I might have a future."

He ran a callused hand down Jacko's neck. "Luke's neighbor wanted to retire to be near their kids. I'd accumulated a lot of pay during the years I was held captive, and I bought his ranch. I had a lot of learning to do, but Luke helped. So did the entire Covenant Falls community. Now I have a wife and two great stepkids along with Jacko. I'll always be grateful to him." He paused. "That's why this program is so important to me. I don't know if I would have discovered a future without him.

"I don't expect that to happen to everyone else," he continued, "or even a few. We can only hope it opens new possibilities and gives them ways to cope with some of the problems." He gave Ross a half smile. "Now let me introduce you to Cajun."

Jacko picked that moment to nuzzled Jubal until he received a carrot.

Jubal's cell phone rang and he answered it. "We're at the stables," he told the caller. "Can you come over here and help show Ross around? Maybe get him on a horse and meet us at the pond."

Some of the tension in Ross's body drained away as Jubal hung up and turned to him. "That was Susan on the phone. She just arrived. Are you ready to join us on the ride?" He didn't wait for an answer and added, "I should catch up with the group, but Danny can get you started with Cajun and then Susan will take over."

Ross hesitated.

Jubal seemed not to notice. "Susan's a good rider and teacher."

Before Ross could reply, Jubal disappeared down the aisle with his horse, leaving Ross thinking black thoughts about the former SEAL. Dammit, he'd been had. Maybe Jubal had sensed his reluctance. Ross hadn't wanted to explain it wasn't the horse he feared. It was the memories.

But wasn't that what this program was all about?

A minute later, Danny appeared with a saddle pad tucked under his arm and a brush in his hand. "Jubal asked me to help you saddle Cajun. He sure is a good horse. He's my favorite. Real easygoing. Nothing ruffles him."

"Where's Hobo?" Ross asked.

"He's in the tack room. Not to worry. The door is closed. I'll get him when Susan gets here."

"You're in this, too," Ross accused him. He was beginning to feel smothered by expectations he'd never anticipated. The plan had been simple. Stay for two weeks or less and make physical therapy recommendations. It certainly hadn't included riding a horse.

"In what, sir?" Danny asked with real puzzlement in his voice.

It had been years since someone had called him "sir."

"Nothing to worry about," Ross said wryly.

Danny put the saddle pad on the stall door. "I'll look after Hobo while you're gone," he said. He added with awe, "He sure is attached to you. He hardly moved until he saw you."

Great! That was all he needed to hear.

"Anything wrong?" the young man asked.

Everything. He had a dog he didn't want, a horse he didn't want to ride and an attraction to a woman he had no business being attracted to. But he couldn't very well admit any of that. He shrugged. "No, just haven't ridden since I was knee-high to a grasshopper," he said. The words popped out. One of his father's favorite expressions. How? Why? He hadn't thought of it in years.

But then waves of memories were washing through him. The night. The next day. The next year. The succeeding years. He closed his eyes for a moment. Then opened them. This barn wasn't anything like the old one that haunted him. This was new and military clean, at least as clean as a barn could be. His family's barn had been old and full of years of smells.

The young veteran slipped a halter on the horse, who neighed and tossed his head as Danny led him out of the stall. He was a chestnut and taller than the other horses he'd seen.

"He's pleased," Danny said.

"How can you tell?"

"You just get to know after a while. He's a social horse. He likes to go out with the others. Danny handed him a brush. "Brush his back before you put the pad on. You don't want anything there that will irritate him while riding. Then you can pick out a saddle in the tack room."

"Sounds good." Ross tried to inject some enthusiasm into his voice. Anything to get the images from his mind. "Jubal tells me you're irreplaceable," He said as he started brushing the horse and tried to ignore the sounds of horses munching or moving in their stalls.

The young man blinked, then broke out in a grin. "Thank you, sir."

"Not me who said it," Ross said, "and there you go with the 'sir' thing. We're not in the army now, and tell that to the others. It's Ross for everyone. And it's Jubal who thinks so highly of you. I don't think he says things like that lightly."

"You knew him when he was in the SEALs?" Danny asked.

"Nope. I was a medic in the Rangers with Josh Manning. I left years before he did."

Ross turned back to brushing Cajun's back, hoping the action would tamp down memories. He'd saddled horses before. He'd stood on a stool and tossed a saddle over his horse, but the horse and saddle were much smaller then…

He finished brushing Cajun and placed the saddle pad in place. Danny, he noted, had left. Cajun nudged him, wanting something in return for his cooperation. Ross ran his hand down Cajun's neck, and the horse nickered back in appreciation.

Ross smiled and leaned against the horse. He'd forgotten how good it felt. Just being with the horse dissipated the lingering shadows inside him. He was beginning to understand the power of the Horses for Heroes programs.

"I sense the beginning of a beautiful friendship."

He turned around. Susan stood there, looking thoughtful.

"You two were communing," she said. "Hate to interrupt but we're supposed to catch up with Luke and

Jubal. Jubal certainly picked the right horse for you. I'm glad it's Cajun."

"Why?" he asked suspiciously. Darn, but she was pretty in a tan shirt and snug jeans. Her brown hair was pulled back in a neat braid.

"I think it hurt his feelings that no one wanted him," she said. "It's his size. It's intimidating for most new riders but just right for you. He's a big softie."

He considered that. Did she mean he was a softie, too? None of his patients thought so.

"Come on," she said. "We'll pick out a saddle for you."

They took Cajun with them toward the tack room and hitched him just outside. Ross looked at the row of saddles on the racks lining the room. Susan went right to a large one and turned. They bumped into each other and his arms went around her to steady her. He caught the gentle whiff of a light flowery scent and their gazes met and held. Damn but her eyes were a fine shade of blue.

For a whisper of time she leaned against him and he had the oddest feeling that she belonged there. But then she pulled away and turned back to the saddle, and he knew he was wrong. She wasn't like the other women he dated. Her commitment to the town and this program was obvious as was the community's obvious affection for her. A fling would never be enough.

"I think this will do," she said in a voice that sounded a bit shaky.

Well, he felt a little shaky, too. "Here," he said. "I'll take it." He needed to get out of the room and into fresh air.

He carried the saddle to where Cajun waited patiently. Ross placed it over the saddle pad, then tightened and buckled the cinch as Susan watched.

"How did I do, Teach?" he asked, making his tone light.

"You didn't need help, after all," she said suspiciously. "How long did you say it's been since you rode?"

"Too many years to count," he replied and then added with a deadpan expression, "But I watch a lot of Westerns, and I know you mount from the left. Or is it the right?"

She raised an eyebrow. "What about the bridle?"

"Oops," he said with his most charming grin. "You mean I can't steer with a halter?"

She gave him a dour look.

"Okay, bridle it is," he assured her.

Under her watchful eyes, he removed the halter and placed the bridle she handed him over Cajun's ears. The horse tried to avoid the bit and closed his mouth tight as Ross's hand neared his mouth—just as Bandit had. *Memories again. These damn memories.*

"Ross?"

Susan's voice snapped him back. His fingers were on the bit but they weren't moving. He breathed slowly again, then saw her concerned face. He took a deep breath and tried again to ease the bit into Cajun's mouth. This time the horse cooperated.

She simply nodded. "Looks good."

Thank God she didn't ask questions, just walked ahead.

He looked down at his hands. There was still a tremor in them. But he'd succeeded. At one time, he'd thought he could never go near a barn or stables again. Well, he'd made it this far.

"You can wait outside and make friends with Cajun

while I saddle Brandy," she said. "She's Lisa's horse, but she shares her with me."

"Can't I help?"

"Nope. I've been doing it since, well, for a long time, and she knows me. Take a carrot or two, and Cajun will be your friend for life."

He did as ordered. He respected competence and she certainly had that. A lot more in horse care than he did. He led Cajun outside, grabbing a carrot from the bucket as he did. He looked ahead as Cajun happily chomped on the treat and nudged him for more. Cajun nudged him again.

"Sorry, kiddo," he said. "You have to wait until we get back. Right now we're waiting for Susan and your friend. Brandy *is* your friend, isn't she? Noncommittal, huh? Good position. Never reveal your cards." He ran his hand over the horse's shoulder. He'd been taught that by his father.

Cajun gave him a horse grin and nudged his chest.

"Okay." Susan's voice came from behind him. He turned and watched her approach. "Stop mooning with each other," she said. "We're running late."

Cajun nodded his head as if agreeing. Or maybe it was just a greeting.

"Can he understand English?" he asked with a raised eyebrow.

"Sometimes I wonder, but I think it's because he's eager to go."

"Are we too late to catch up?" he asked.

"We don't have to," she replied. "They'll either be at the pond or on their way back, and we'll meet them."

He turned and looked at her. No businesswoman now.

Riding gloves peeked out of her jeans' pocket, and her riding boots were old and scuffed. She looked all cowgirl.

"I'm playing hooky from the inn," she said. "The last few weeks were really busy, and now I intend to relax and enjoy being part of this. I love seeing these guys start to unwind. Wait until tonight. They'll probably be a little sore, but they've survived the first two days and there's usually music and fun."

She swung up into the saddle, and he followed, wondering whether he would make a damn fool out of himself. Then he settled himself into the saddle and hoped Jubal was right about people never forgetting how to ride.

Chapter 6

"Luke and Jubal want to see how each one of this group rides," Susan explained as she turned toward the trail pointed out to Ross earlier. "Luke checked them out yesterday in the ring but he wants to see how well they do outside it and what kind of advanced instruction they want or need." She paused, then asked, "Feel like trying to catch up?"

He nodded.

She knew he would. Throw out a dare to a military guy and he was going to take it every time.

After several minutes, she turned to him. "You have a fair seat for a motorcycle jockey," she noted.

He grinned. "What do you have against motorcycles?"

He'd apparently noticed her lack of enthusiasm for his choice of vehicle. She just plain didn't like the damn things. A close cousin died on one. She knew the grief it cost her family.

"They're dangerous," she replied.

"So are horses if you don't know what you're doing," he said.

"It's more likely you'll get killed on a motorcycle."

"Not if you know what you're doing," he threw back at her.

"Do you go everywhere on one?"

"Mostly. Have you ever ridden one?"

"No," she admitted. "I don't have a death wish."

"Then you wouldn't know the freedom you don't feel anywhere else," he said with that wry grin that set off a flurry of reactions inside her. "With a bike, you're riding the wind."

"I get that feeling on a horse," she argued.

"Not the same. You'll have to ride a bike to understand."

She didn't get it and had no intention of proving or disproving it herself. In any event it was none of her business. His safety on the horse was. She turned all her attention to that.

He had a natural seat and moved easily with the animal. Of course, Cajun was probably the most rideable of the unselected horses despite his size, and Ross was obviously both a natural and a trained athlete.

She noticed he was light on the reins and she didn't know if it was remembered from long ago or just instinct. He'd been a little hesitant at first but he was catching on fast. She suspected the hesitation came from doing something he wasn't sure he was mastering.

She smiled at the remembered image of his frustration in her bathroom.

He gave her a questioning look. "Am I that bad a rider?"

"No. I was thinking of last night and wondering who was giving who a bath."

A pained expression passed over his face. "I'm trying to forget it. I told your friend Danny not to let Hobo near a mud puddle."

She laughed. Had it just been last night when they first met? It seemed they'd known each other longer. Much longer. She tried to concentrate on the here and now. "Actually, your posture is good. You might hold the reins a little tighter. Let Cajun know you're in control."

"He seems to know where he's going. I think he has a crush on your mare."

"Well, he might see another lady along the way, one he likes better, and take off."

"That doesn't sound very gentlemanly of him."

"You never know about the male species," she retorted with a smile. "He just might decide to test you."

"Okay." He tightened the reins. They were moving at a fast walk now.

"How long has it been since you rode?" she asked.

He shrugged. "Not since I was a kid."

Her curiosity was aroused now. "How old?"

"Ten."

"Why not since then?"

"A few things, like the army, college, graduate school." His voice was nearly toneless now. She knew the sound. She'd heard it from some of the vets when they talked about combat. There was a lot he wasn't saying, but an inner voice warned her against pursuing that particular subject.

Her curiosity had grown stronger since this morning. He'd shaved and his face was deeply tanned. His sandy blond hair glimmered in the sun, and his eyes appeared a darker gray. His body had a grace to it, even now on a horse he didn't know.

Quit it, Susan. He's a rolling stone. You're a monument. "How do you feel about a faster pace?" she asked. "A slow trot, not a gallop."

"I'm game." The uncertainty was gone. He was sitting a little taller and she'd noticed he'd been watching her hands and following suit. He was a quick study, or maybe it was remembered. She wondered about his slight hesitancy just before he mounted. He didn't seem to be the kind of man who hesitated.

She rode beside him, noting the smile that started to stretch across his face. Riding did the same for her, especially on a fine fall day with a cloudless sky and the hint of a breeze. Hells bells, but he was a fine-looking man. Not handsome in the traditional way, but there was a quiet strength.

Josh thought highly of him. She was beginning to understand why. He was a big man with a gentle heart. She saw it in the way he treated Hobo, in the way he respected others, even in the way he'd run his fingers down Cajun's neck before mounting. Small but telling things. But there was also a reserve. She sensed he didn't let anyone get too close to him.

Her breath caught as they glanced at each other at the same second. Their gazes held for an instant. Awareness flashed between them. Her heart beat faster and her breath caught somewhere in her throat. She forced herself to look ahead. She'd never believed in the myth of two strangers whose glances met across a crowded room, and they knew at that second the other was the person for them. It only happened in novels and movies.

No one, she reminded herself, could know the character of that person in one instant. No one could know their weaknesses. They might be serial killers for all one knew. She swallowed hard. She'd learned caution the hard way. Still, she couldn't deny the attraction, that there was a spark between them, a powerful one that shot through her body. Hells bells, it was already fire and headed toward an explosion.

She'd warned herself against spending time with him, but she'd agreed fast enough when Josh asked her to drive him to Jubal's ranch. She could have pled inn business or personal business, but Josh would know that to be a lie. She had no personal business other than the inn and the New Beginnings program.

That was sad. She hadn't thought so until now. She'd been perfectly content with her life. Content with her friends and her job and her projects.

Content with *safe* after years of turmoil.

She still was, she told herself. She didn't want anything to change. She certainly didn't want to be attracted to a stranger who was going to leave in a week or two. That was especially true now that she learned he worked with the rich and famous.

He was around beautiful people just as her ex-husband had been. It had been seductive until it became a nightmare. How could Covenant Falls compete with Los Angeles? He could never be interested in staying in a small town that had no hospital, no gyms, and not much of anything but scenery and good people. And she wasn't going to leave again. Everything she loved was here.

But then, no was asking her to leave.

Susan took a deep breath. *Just think about the party tonight and making it good for the guests.*

"Susan?" His glance was curious.

She shrugged off her thoughts. "Just thinking about tonight. You'll meet more of the veterans who moved here. Clint, a former chopper pilot turned police chief, will entertain. He plays a mean guitar and has a repertoire of cowboy songs."

"And you? What's your role tonight?"

"None. I can sit back and enjoy."

"Ha," he said. "I suspect you will be in the middle of everything, trying to make everyone feel comfortable."

"I think they already do."

"Maybe not yet, but they will in another week or two."

She'd been intrigued by him last night because of his dogged determination to do things he appeared to not want to do. And he did it with a sense of humor. She liked men who didn't take themselves too seriously. She'd been married to someone who always had to win, even if he cheated to do so.

"How did you get roped into being here all day?" he asked.

"I love it," she said. "How can you beat being outside on a day like this? Sun shining. Good horse. People I like. A party tonight. It always starts a little stiff but when Clint starts playing the guitar, accompanied by a cowboy from Luke's ranch who plays harmonica, everyone loosens up. Before long they're all calling out songs."

She paused, then asked, "Question is how did *you* get roped into it?" It seemed each time she learned something about him, there were more questions.

"Josh asked," he said simply.

"That simple?" She was being intrusive but she couldn't stop herself.

"I served with Josh. There was never a better leader,

and he saved a bunch of lives, mine among them. A lot of us owe him."

"How did you become a physical therapist?"

"As a Ranger medic, I saw far too many injuries. All I could do was patch them up with what little I had and send them on." He shrugged. "It was damned frustrating. I decided to get my BSc degree and go for a doctorate in physical therapy. I'd accumulated a number of college credits online and received credit for military courses and experience. It took two more years to get my degree, then another three for my doctorate. I'd just finished a job when Josh called, so it was also good timing.

"Where were you?"

"California."

"Is that where you practice?" she asked.

"I don't have one place. I'm what you call a per diem or traveling physical therapist. I don't work with one facility or business. I'm basically an independent contractor. I can choose cases and locations. Sometimes it's filling in at a VA facility or city hospital. Sometimes it's an individual patient. Basically, it gives me a freedom I wouldn't otherwise have."

"Like the bike does?" she said.

He smiled. "Yeah. Like that."

"Where do you call home?" she asked.

"I don't," he said bluntly.

"No home base?"

"No."

He'd told her as much before, but it was so odd. Surely even a wanderer had someplace to hang his hat, to be at Christmas or keep belongings. You must live somewhere."

"Why?"

"Everyone does."

"I'm not everyone."

He most definitely was not. He was more clam than human when it came to personal information. She had to drag everything out, and she was usually good at that. He was a challenge.

"But you must have a house or apartment or boat or office. Something for legal purposes." She couldn't help herself from persisting. It had become a challenge to learn more, not only more, but why.

He shrugged. "A friend handles that for me. I use his address for bank cards, driver's license and the few bills that come in. He also keeps equipment I might need and can send for. He can always get in touch with me." He hesitated, then added, "It doesn't make much sense to either buy or rent if I'm never there."

"Doesn't it get lonely?"

"Nope," he replied simply. "There's always new and interesting people to meet."

"I can understand that," she said.

"I thought you could," he said.

"But don't you have family somewhere?"

"No," he said simply.

The flatness of the answer did not invite more questions but she couldn't leave it alone. It seemed sad and lonely to her. She had a mom in Covenant Falls and a couple of aunts. She had six cousins, only one that still lived locally but the others visited often.

They should try to catch up to the other riders, but she wanted to know more. "Then where in California were you last?"

"Los Angeles."

"Where were you born?"

He looked at her with a raised eyebrow. "About a hundred miles south of here."

"Ranch country," she said. "Or were you a townie?"

"We're going to miss the others," he said.

She knew pressing him was not going to yield any results and it really wasn't her business but she'd never met anyone so completely rootless.

Darn Josh for being his usual taciturn self and omitting a great deal of information when he'd told her Ross was staying at the inn. But even if he had explained more about his friend, she didn't think she would have been prepared for his slow smile and easygoing manner. Except when it came to his personal life.

She changed the subject. "Think you're ready for a slow trot?"

"I do," he said. Ross sounded relieved to leave behind the topic of his residence or lack thereof.

"Just tighten your knees against his side," she said. They soon caught up with Luke and Jubal's group, who had stopped at the side of a pond.

She listened as Jubal talked to the vets. He apparently had been waiting for the two of them to arrive. She knew it all, and more, but Ross didn't. "New Beginnings has around fifty acres," Jubal said. "Luke, here, has nearly a hundred and leases more. He and his wife run cattle as well as raising and training quarter horses. Toward the end of this program you'll have a chance to work the cattle if you're so inclined.

"I have two pastures. One is for the riding horses. They go out every night and return the next morning. Beyond that is the pasture for mares and young offspring. They stay together."

Jubal continued as his audience listened intently.

"There's a path from here that goes up into the mountains. In the last week, we'll take pack horses up there. It leads to an abandoned gold camp. There's several of them around us. All of you should already have had survival training, but we'll review it.

"In the meantime, we want you to spend time with your horse even when you're not riding or in class.

"When Luke thinks you're ready, you can ride on my property without one of us along, but not alone. I want at least two of you together. Got it?"

"Ross Taylor will meet with each of you this week and suggest programs that will help your riding and physical health."

Jubal looked up at the sun. "It's time to go back. Anyone uncomfortable with a trot—or maybe a canter?"

Two raised hands. "Good," Luke said. "There's no shame in admitting what you don't know, only if you don't let either Jubal or me know about it. You're here to learn as well as enjoy. We don't expect you to be expert riders today. We do expect you to be good ones in six weeks.

"Adam and Carl," he said to the two who had raised their hands, "you ride back with Susan and Ross. You're lucky. You get to ride with Susan instead of me." He then led his group into a fast pace toward the bunkhouse.

"Come on, guys," Susan said. "They may have speed but we'll have a nice leisurely walk, then a slow trot. The doc here is a beginner, too."

She saw him wince at the word "doc" and grinned at him. It would stick now. She knew it. He knew it.

They didn't talk on the ride back. Susan was too occupied with the two other riders and making sure they didn't get into equine trouble.

She didn't worry about Ross. He wasn't completely

at ease on horseback yet, but she trusted Cajun. She did worry about herself. She'd never met anyone like Ross Taylor before. He was a contradiction: a loner who melded seamlessly with others.

As if he knew she was thinking about him, he moved next to her. "Do you ever slow down?"

"Not when I love what I'm doing," she replied.

Dammit, but his eyes were challenging. She was as helpless against them as she was against that sheepish grin in her bathroom. "Let's try a trot," she told her three companions. We'll take it slow. Just relax in the saddle."

She was grateful when they finally reached the stables. "You did great," she told the three.

The two young vets beamed. Ross simply raised an eyebrow.

"Cool off the horses and rub them down before leaving," she said. "When you finish, a nice reward for your horse is in order." She knew they would have been told about the bottomless bucket of carrots.

"Yes, ma'am," one of them said. She remembered his name was Carl.

"Make that Susan," she said.

"Yes, ma'am, I mean Susan," Carl said, and blushed to his scalp before leading his horse into the stable.

She glanced at Ross. He was watching her with a small smile.

She wasn't surprised when Ross dismounted and led Cajun inside. He did everything right. It was incredibly frustrating.

In fact, he was probably the most frustrating man she'd ever met. And, damn it, the most interesting.

Chapter 7

Maybe you never do forget how to ride, as Jubal claimed.

As Ross cooled Cajun down and gave him his carrot, he realized he knew each step without prompting. Apparently, they *had* been imprinted on him when he was young.

The stable here looked nothing like the old barn his family owned, nor did the rich green grass look like the often-dry, inhospitable ground where he'd grown up.

But now he allowed himself to remember the joy of riding Bandit before everything came to an end.

After feeding Cajun, Ross walked over to the bunkhouse area while Susan stayed inside the stable to help the vets. Lawn chairs and camp chairs were scattered in front of the building.

The inviting scent of grilling meat had lured both program participants and visitors over to the cooking area.

Josh was at the grill with several younger guys. When he saw Ross, he left them and hurried over.

"How's your stepson?" Ross asked.

"The arm wasn't broken. Just sprained. In fact, he insisted on coming tonight. Heard you rode today. How did it go?"

"Better than I expected," Ross said. "Are they feeding an army?" he asked, staring at mounds of meat—burgers, hot dogs and sausages—on a table next to the grill.

"Oh, there will be more people here. Our families. The other program volunteers and some area ranchers who help us out. That reminds me," he added, "I make some mean steaks. You'll have to come over this week and try one."

"I would like that."

Josh gave him a searching look. "Good. I know you're holding a meeting tomorrow evening with all the guys so we'll try for Tuesday." He paused, then added, "Heard you went for a ride with Susan."

"And other vets," Ross said.

"Now that most of the inn guests are gone, she'll probably spend more time out here."

Ross looked at his friend with suspicion. "Don't get any ideas, Josh. I like what you're doing here, and I like Susan, but I'm not staying beyond two weeks."

"Not to worry," Josh replied. "Just want you to have a good time while you're here." Then he added, "It would be great if you can come back toward the end of the six-week program and see how we've progressed. Maybe even go on the final trip."

Ross raised an eyebrow. "Remember, I know you," he said. "You have few scruples when you think something is important to 'your' guys. I take it that these are 'your' guys now."

Just then, Danny emerged from the bunkhouse with Hobo limping behind him. The little dog made straight for Ross, hobbling as best he could and making throaty noises. His tail wagged. It was more activity than he'd seen from the dog.

Ross reached down and picked him up. "Hey, there. Doing okay?"

Hobo stuck out a tongue and licked his hand. More little throaty noises.

"Getting fresh now?" Ross said to the dog. He looked back up at Josh. "That's the first time he's made those noises."

"Maybe he feels safe for the first time," Ross said.

"That's sad," Danny said.

"Yeah, it is," Josh interceded. "He was lucky you saw him," he added. "By the way, my family should be here soon. They'll be bringing Amos."

"I'm still amazed you found Amos," Ross said.

"It took a while. The army was loath to let him go, but he had PTSD as bad as any soldier. He really mourned David, would barely come out from under the bed for weeks. But now he loves my stepson and Nick's collection of animal misfits. Amos looks after them as if they were his own, and I guess they are."

"You look happy."

"I am. You ought to try marriage sometime."

"Nope. I like my life just as it is."

Josh shrugged. "One of these days…but in the meantime, why don't you check out the bunkhouse, then you can circulate and meet the rest of our veterans. You did get the list of them with what personal and medical information I had?"

"Jubal gave it to me earlier. I suspect I'll be up all night reading it."

"We hope to add some physically disabled vets in our next program. These guys have PTSD and other military caused problems." Josh turned to Danny. "Can you show Ross the bunkhouse? I should stay out here."

Ross nodded and he and Danny turned toward the bunkhouse, Hobo limping between them. "I was thinking maybe he should stay in the bunkhouse," Ross said. "Place needs a dog."

"There's not always someone here," Danny said. "And he apparently thinks he's your dog."

"Just can't happen. I travel too much for work."

Danny looked disappointed but proudly showed him around the bunkhouse. "I helped build it," he said. "Nearly half the town came over and had an old-fashioned barn raising. Food and all," he added with enthusiasm that belied his thin form. "I learned a lot about construction."

Ross was impressed. The bunkhouse was plain but comfortable. There were basically three rooms. Two were sleeping rooms with bunk beds, a large one for men and a smaller one for women. Each had their own bath areas. Located between them was the largest room, a gathering area with a small kitchen, long dining room table and mismatched but comfortable chairs and sofas.

For entertainment there was a Ping-Pong table, a bookcase stacked with titles ranging from horse care to Western novels and mysteries, and table games. Workout equipment sat in another corner.

"There's no phones or television allowed," Danny said,

"although they can contact their families every Saturday and, of course, if there's an emergency. I think that's the most difficult part for some, but it's really important that they interact with each other and their horses without distractions."

During the few hours before the cookout, Ross met with most of the participants. They varied in age from early twenties to over forty. He hadn't had a chance yet to read their histories from the book Jubal had given him, but the brief meetings revealed some of the problems: PTSD, night sweats, panic attacks, alcohol abuse, drug abuse, joblessness.

He asked about their exercise routines, if there were any. None had.

Yet.

"What about a run at sunrise?" he suggested to each one and had several takers. "Tell the others, okay? It's completely voluntary. I'll be outside here at 6:00 a.m. for whoever wants to go."

As the evening went on, the number of people outside multiplied. Several of the vets were returning from riding lessons or simply talking to their horses. Others headed for the bunkhouse, probably to clean up before the cookout. He looked at the extended family of Covenant Falls veterans that were doing something about a need far greater than most people understood. It filled him with pride.

It didn't hurt that the sun was providing a great backdrop as it descended toward the mountains. He smiled as he listened to the voices of invigorated vets talking excitedly about their equine adventures.

Just days ago, some of them probably couldn't leave their homes.

He'd volunteered with veteran rehab facilities both during and after getting his degree. He was only too aware of the fears, the nightmares, the flashbacks, the loneliness that kept them from living normal lives. Many returned to a community and friends with little understanding of what they'd experienced and were still experiencing. The comradery here was as important as learning equine skills.

A boy of perhaps fifteen walked up to him. His arm was in a sling. "I'm Nick," he said. "Josh's son," he added. "I'm proud to meet you, sir."

"And I'm happy to meet you," Ross replied. "I hear you're an animal guru." The boy stooped down to greet Hobo.

"He's a great dog," Nick said as he hugged the dog.

"Every dog is great to Nick," interrupted a tall attractive woman. "I'm Eve, Josh's wife. But no more animals for us," she added before Nick could make an offer. "Why don't you get a hamburger?" she said to her son and shooed him off. "It's really good to meet you," she said. "Josh was delighted when you agreed to come."

"Delighted?" Ross asked wryly. "It's difficult to tell with Josh."

"No one can," she replied. "Josh doesn't show much emotion but he's been talking about you for the last month. He's really impressed by what you've done, getting a doctorate in physical therapy.

"How did he even know?"

"The Rangers," she said. "That's one powerful grapevine. A former member of your unit was in the first session we had here. He'd met you when you helped out at a veteran's event. He passed the word to us. Hunting you down was not easy."

Ross shrugged. "Josh may be impressed, but I'm awe-struck. A businessman, inn owner and cofounder of this program. Was that all your doing?"

She shook her head. "I'm just along for the ride," she said.

"I doubt that."

"I hope I see a lot of you," Eve said. "Now I'd better go over and make sure my son is getting salad as well as tons of everything that's bad for him."

As if on cue, Susan approached with a big grin. She held a plate full of food. He wondered how her figure remained perfect. Probably because she never stopped moving. "You look empty handed," she observed. "I would have brought you supper, but I don't know what you like."

He looked at her plate. "Everything you have," he said, "but I'll get it."

"I'll guard your chair."

He looked around. The area was filling up. "How many vets have moved here recently?" he asked. "They seem to be popping up everywhere."

"Five in the past two and a half years."

"They're all married now?"

"Yeah," she said with that quick smile of hers. "Odd, isn't it?"

"All to Covenant Falls people?"

"Except for the last couple. They met here about eight months ago. Travis was just getting out of rehab after two years of surgeries when Josh asked him to do a study on Horses for Heroes programs and he traveled to different programs throughout the West. A reporter, Jenny, kind of forced her way into the trip. She'd been injured in Syria while covering a story and was trying to find one here in the States. They fell in love while research-ing this project."

He shook his head. "I need a diagram to get every-one straight."

"They're all very different," she said. "The first was Josh. When he married the mayor, he wanted his cabin to go to another vet that needed it, and that turned out to be a battlefield surgical nurse who'd lost her fiancé and the use of her hand in Afghanistan. She married a native of Covenant Falls, a builder who joined with Josh to build the inn. Then the cabin went to a chopper pilot, Clint, who fell in love with Stephanie, a veterinarian."

"Is there something in the water here?" Ross asked only a little skeptically. *God help me, I've had several glasses of it.*

Susan continued, "Everyone helped with the program in one way or another. They'd all had varying degrees of PTSD. Everything just started fitting together."

"And you?"

"I'd moved back to Covenant Fall after being gone for a long time," she explained. "I was looking for a job when Josh started thinking about building an inn. He and Eve wanted the town to grow, but few people even knew it existed. The last mayor wanted it that way. Eve got herself elected and started a revival."

"And you?" he asked. "Why did you come back?"

She hesitated, then shrugged. "It was time. My roots are here."

From the way she said it, he knew there was a story behind the statement.

He also realized from her tone that she didn't want to continue the subject.

"I *am* hungry," he said. "And I should get up before

those aches you warned me about set in. Can you watch out for Hobo?"

"Sure. We're becoming good buddies. And it's a good idea for you to keep moving."

"I run a lot. Shouldn't have a problem."

"As a physical therapist, you should know you probably used muscles today even you haven't tested recently."

"Want to place a small bet?"

"What do you want to wager?"

"A dog?" he said hopefully.

"You're not getting rid of him that easily."

Ross sighed. It was worth a try. "I should get food before it's all gone," he said before he blurted out something stupid. "Can I get you anything else?" he asked.

"I'm fine," she said.

He introduced himself to the man standing at the grill—who turned out to be Clint—and helped himself. He was starved and filled his plate with a huge cheeseburger, a brat sandwich, salad, potato salad, baked beans and two brownies.

"That's what I like to see," Clint said. "Someone who eats as much as I do. Welcome to Covenant Falls."

"I hear your wife is the local veterinarian," Ross said. "I have a dog that needs some medical attention. And a permanent home."

"She's just arrived home after a search and rescue that ended badly. She could be here later, but don't get your hopes up. She's not taking in any more rescues at the moment but she would be happy to check out your dog."

"He's not my dog," Ross insisted as he noticed Hobo had followed him.

"Looks like he thinks differently," Clint said. "I mean,

dogs usually pick their owner, and it looks like he picked you. I noticed he stays right at your feet."

Ross narrowed his eyes. "Not you, too."

Clint grinned. "What is, is," he said cryptically. "You can yell and protest and fight it all you want, but you won't win." With that sage advice, he added, "Enjoy your food" and turned to talk to one of the young vets manning the grill with him.

Ross grabbed a glass of lemonade and returned to his chair with his stacked plate. Hobo crawled over to get as close as possible to him.

Thankfully, Susan didn't seem to notice as he took a bite of his cheeseburger. Instead, she glanced at his plate with a raised eyebrow. "Hungry, are we?"

"Yes, and we are keeping it to ourselves," he replied as Hobo looked up at him longingly.

Ross took another big bite, then looked back down at Hobo, who was staring at him intently. He groaned. "I have to get him some proper dog food."

"That would probably be a good idea," she said. "That's why I bought several cans as well as a leash and collar. You owe me twenty-seven dollars plus change."

"I'll make a trade. Hobo for that twenty-seven dollars," he suggested.

"I have a cat that would never tolerate him, remember?" She smiled. "And I'll tell you something else. I think you want him, too, even if you won't admit it."

He raised one eyebrow. "I'm *not* keeping him despite any conspiracies to the contrary."

But Susan was right. Maybe part of him did want the dog. Problem was Hobo reminded him of the past—of Patches, his dog and best friend, who disappeared on the same day he lost everything else—and threatened the future he'd worked so hard to build.

He took another bite of his food. It suddenly tasted like sand. He looked downward and saw large brown eyes gazing back with longing. No begging. No whining. Just hope. He sighed and gave Hobo a piece of his sandwich, then sat back and became an onlooker again.

Ross was ready to call it a night when Clint picked up a guitar and started strumming.

The sun was gone now, leaving only a halo over the mountain. In the other direction a nearly full moon was rising. The breeze quickened and rippled through the pines.

He looked at Susan. Her attention was riveted on Clint, a smile on her face as he started singing, but he quickly realized it was the music that drew her. The ex-chopper pilot was good. He sang mostly cowboy songs, concentrating on those that told stories about outlaws or cattle drives.

At the end of his last song, Jubal made an announcement. "Now that all of you survived your first ride on a horse here," he said, "we have first grade graduation presents."

"Bring them out, Danny," he added.

Beaming, Danny uncovered a wheelbarrow full of new cowboy hats. There was a collective cheer. "These are from the merchants in town," Jubal said. "Between you and me I think they want you to stay in Covenant Falls and enrich them but, for the moment, enjoy."

Ross watched the vets rush over to select their hats and try them on. A lot of ribbing was exchanged as they bartered back and forth. He couldn't help but smile.

A pretty girl of around fifteen approached. "You must

be Mr. Taylor," she said. "I've met everyone else. I've been helping out at Dr. Morgan's office today since she's been out."

"I'm Ross Taylor, usually the dreaded physical therapist," he admitted. And you are…?" he asked.

"I'm Lisa's sister, Kerry. That makes me Jubal's sister-in-law or something." She knelt beside Hobo. "Who is this?"

"An orphan looking for a home," he said, even as he caught Susan's disapproving frown.

"We already have two," Kerry said, "and a bunch of horses. What happened to his leg?"

"Someone shot him," he said. "I found him on the road. I hope to see Stephanie tomorrow."

"She should be in the office early." Kerry leaned down and ran her hand over Hobo's body and received a lick in appreciation. "He looks awfully thin."

"Yes, he does," Ross said. "But he's been eating well lately. Extremely well," he added as Hobo snatched a part of a sausage that fell from his plate.

Kerry's eyes cleared. "That's good. Pleased to meet you, Mr. Taylor."

She left and continued to circle the crowd.

"She's a good kid," Susan said. "So is her brother. He's almost nineteen now and has turned into a good riding instructor."

"So Jubal now has a wife and two teenagers."

"It's a case of never say never," Susan said with the grin that was so contagious.

"Explain," he said.

"The last thing Jubal wanted when he came here was a family."

"What happened?"

"He claims there's magic here in the mountains," Susan said. "So does Josh."

"In addition to the water?" he asked ironically.

She looked at him curiously. "Water?"

"Never mind. It was just a thought. But Josh? He's the most down-to-earth, practical guy I've ever met," Ross said. "What kind of magic?"

"I'll have to show you while you're here."

He raised an eyebrow. "When?"

"Maybe tomorrow or the next day. It'll take a few hours."

"Do you ever slow down?"

She shrugged. "I think I'm running on adrenaline now."

He looked at his watch. It was nearly nine and he had no idea when she'd left her house this morning except he knew it was before 7:00 a.m. "I should get back to the inn. I want to read the notes Travis made during his scouting trip."

"I'll drive you," she said. "I think most of the volunteers are leaving now. It's been a long day for our vets and I imagine they would like some time to unwind."

He agreed. They'd had a lot thrown at them today. He suspected they needed some time to talk among themselves.

"Should I look after Cajun?" he asked, recalling the rule about taking care of one's horse.

"No. This was a one ride thing. Danny will feed the horses that weren't selected by the vets and put them out to the pasture."

"I'll tell Jubal we're leaving," he said, "and pick up the research material."

She nodded. "You'll be one of the few guests at the

inn and we're cutting back on staff. Can you do with less service?"

"Since it's free, I think I can manage."

"Not exactly free since you're working for it," she reminded him. "I'll take Hobo and meet you at the Jeep."

He found Jubal and walked with him to get the book he'd mentioned along with information about each of the vets. "I thought I would take the vets on a sunrise run," he said. "It will give me an idea of their fitness if they participate and their lack of drive if they don't."

"Sounds good," Jubal responded. "I might join you."

"Probably better if you don't. I want them relaxed. If you come, they would want to try to outrun a Navy SEAL. Maybe later."

Jubal nodded. "I get that." He changed the subject. "How do you like the inn?"

"In all of the ten minutes I spent in the room, it looks great."

"Need a ride back?"

"Susan offered to drive me."

An odd expression flashed across Jubal's face.

Ross didn't know him well enough to read it, but it renewed some suspicions he had.

Ross took the material and headed for the parking area. They—the whole contriving group—were wrong if they thought he was joining their ranks. He could smell a setup a mile away. He had his own goals.

He'd planned out the lifestyle he wanted since the day he left the army. A small town in the middle of nowhere sure as hell wasn't included.

Chapter 8

Susan was only too aware of the man sitting next to her as she drove. He smelled like horse but so did she. She liked it. Preferred it, in fact, to most aftershave lotions and perfumes.

She hadn't known what to think when she first saw him.

Today she'd seen the power of his smile and his ability to bond with people. Whether it was young Danny or an awkward, uncertain veteran who'd gone through hell, he'd made them feel comfortable and like the most important person around.

Despite his efforts to pawn little Hobo off on someone else, he handled him with gentleness. It had made her heart jump a bit to see such a large man be so gentle with a homely, wounded animal. She understood now why the dog trusted him.

"You're being quiet," he said.

"I'm winding down," she said. She paused, then asked, "What do you think?"

"Of the program?"

"Yes."

"It's still a work in progress," he said. "Both Josh and Jubal know it. They're open to ideas. I like the fact there's enough volunteers to give each of the participants confidence and support. I would like to see more psychiatric input and ongoing physical therapy. But that's the ideal.

"I'm starting a mile run every morning at sunrise," he continued. "It's voluntary. Any ideas about a route?"

"Just turn left when you leave the gate," she replied. "There's just a few ranches on that end of the road, and very little traffic. It sounds like a great idea."

"I'm hoping all of them will eventually join me and by the end of the program it'll be an ingrained part of their life."

"Can I join it?" she asked.

"I expect you would be an added incentive. I might even have full participation on the first try."

She shook her head in denial.

He raised an eyebrow. "You don't notice the way they all seek your approval?"

"I don't think…"

He sought a new topic. "Have you always lived here?"

"No," she said.

There was a pause, then he asked the question she didn't want to answer. "Where else?"

"I was in Las Vegas for several years"

"That's about as far from here as you could get," he observed, "and I don't mean in miles."

"I worked for a hotel there," she said. "And," she

added almost defiantly, "I was married and divorced there." She might as well get that out now. Everyone in town knew it, which meant he would probably hear it. Why would it matter anyway? He was only going to be here thirteen more days, but who was counting?

"Somehow I can't picture you in that atmosphere."

"Neither can I. *Now.* It's a long sad story for another time," she said as she drove up to the inn. "Is there anything we—the inn—can do for you since you were treated so poorly last night?"

"I don't think I was treated badly, especially since I didn't warn you I would be late," he said. "But there *is* something you can do."

"Name it."

"A pillowcase."

"A pillowcase?" she asked with a puzzled look. "They're on the bed."

"A spare one," he explained. "One you don't need back so I can make it into a sling."

"For Hobo?" she guessed.

"Until I find him a proper home," he explained. "I don't want to leave him in the room alone, and I don't want to ride my bike onto the ranch and scare the horses. Nor do I want you to have to ferry us back and forth. I plan to make a sling for Hobo and run over there. It's not much over two miles."

"And then you want to run another mile and back with our vets?"

"I enjoy running," he explained, "particularly in the morning. It's a routine with me."

"And you create slings, as well. A man of many talents."

"I was a medic. You would be surprised at the creativity that's required."

"Okay," she agreed. "I'll bring a pillowcase. Anything else? Scissors? Thread? Needle?"

"Nope. That will do it."

Susan parked the Jeep. The parking lot looked lonely tonight after weeks of being full. Only five other cars were there. She reached in the backseat and handed him a package. "A gift for Hobo. He had excellent behavior today."

He started for his wallet in his jeans. "You said twenty-seven dollars."

"I changed my mind. I'm gifting him, not you."

"Well, maybe in the next few days he'll gift you."

She frowned at him. "He'll do no such thing."

They went into the front entrance together, then he and Hobo peeled off to the left to his room and she went to the desk.

Janet, a widow and part-timer, was on desk duty on Sunday evening, usually the slowest time. She would stay at the desk until the last guest came in and retired. Then she was free to use the room behind the reception area. There was a comfortable cot and a restroom and, on a slow night, the night clerk was permitted to nap. There was a bell on the front desk for guest requests.

Janet was reading a romance as she usually did when holding down the fort. "A couple came in several hours ago. A walk-in. They're taking a road trip and read about us in a tourist magazine. Then we have the two couples who prolonged their stay to take the Jeep trip to the gold mine and stopped at the waterfall. They had dinner at Maude's and are in for the night. They seemed happy. We have ten new reservations, seven for next weekend."

"All in one day?"

"Yep. The phone's been ringing."

"That's great. Can you stay until ten tomorrow? Mark will take over then."

Sure."

"You don't know how much I appreciate all of you putting in extra hours these past few weeks," she said. "I know it's been crazy busy."

"You don't know how much we appreciate the jobs," Janet replied. "Until the vets came, there wasn't much here."

Susan nodded, then went into the linen room and selected a pillowcase along with some small bags from a box. She made a stop in the kitchen stockroom and grabbed a bottle of the red wine they offered guests in the afternoon. She took it all to Ross's room.

She knocked, and the door opened almost immediately. Ross had taken his T-shirt off and the visual was outstanding. She tried to take her gaze away from the finest chest she'd ever seen. Not overly muscled, just solid and brick hard and tanned and... She wondered for half a second how it would feel next to her.

Dammit. Hadn't she learned her lesson yet? She shoved the pillowcase and bottle of wine at him, then handed him some of the little bags. "For Hobo," she said, hoping he didn't need more explanation. "As for the wine, it's for the room mix-up. I don't know if you drink it but..."

"I do," he said, "and thank you. For that, for the ride, for your help today."

"Welcome to Covenant Falls," she said. "Just let us know if you need anything. Good night. I hope you sleep well." It sounded terribly formal. She felt like a total fool.

She was thirty-six years old and she was probably blushing as if she'd never seen a man's chest before.

But, darn it, he was gorgeous. She could ignore that, but what was worse he seemed to be a really good guy. The combination was dangerous. She bit her lip. She hadn't done that in years.

"Will you have a glass of wine?" he asked. "I don't like to drink by myself."

No. "Yes," she said. She walked over to the window. The moon was a big round ball tonight. It seemed to be glowing just for her. But that was nonsense.

As he joined her, she turned, took a half-full glass from him, then looked up into silver gray eyes. Her breath caught in her throat. A rush of heat ran through her body. She forced herself to take a step away. *He's leaving in less than two weeks.* She kept telling herself that.

That fact was both an enticement and a warning. The enticement was she wouldn't get deeply involved in two weeks. The warning was maybe she would. She'd thought her ex-husband was a good guy. He'd been her mentor, her guide through the perilous journey of politics in a major hotel—until he wasn't.

Ross's fingers touched her face and played along her cheekbones, stoking little fires that streaked through her body. The restrained caress was more sensual than demanding.

An ache started deep inside her, a gnawing, needy ache. She knew she should move away. A relationship, any relationship, was too risky on several accounts. But the tenderness of his hand erased her instinct to flee.

He pulled her toward him and their gazes met, questioned. A sizzling wave of heat ran through her as he leaned down, his lips brushing hers. They were tentative at first, searching, then his kiss grew in intensity. The core of her warmed, and she found herself craving more. She went up on tiptoe to better fit into his arms. Every nerve in her seemed to come alive.

His lips caressed hers. They were searching at first, then more demanding. But even as she leaned into him, her body nestling against his, she kept finding reasons to pull back.

He was a wanderer. He'd made that plain almost from the moment they had met. Could she risk falling in love? She wasn't there yet but knew if this went further she could be. All too easily.

From the beginning, there had been a connection that sizzled between them. It had, she realized, been building between them since they met last night. It strengthened with the easy companionship during their horseback ride together. There had been glances, quickly diverted.

He leaned down and kissed her, then suddenly straightened, but his hand lingered on her face. "You're one hell of a woman," he said.

She looked up at him, ran her fingers over the strong lines of his face. She thought of all his kindnesses. Under that fierce exterior and daunting size, there was a tender heart. She witnessed it many times today in small and big ways. The run tomorrow was just another example. By making it voluntary, he was giving the vets respect.

Her heart pounded.

"Ditto," she said, "I mean if I substitute 'you' for 'me,' and 'man' for 'woman' and…"

She stopped abruptly and analyzed what she'd just said. "That doesn't make sense, does it?"

He chuckled. "Yeah, it does." He leaned down and his lips trailed kisses down her face. Heat was growing between them again, their eyes locked on each other. "I would love to take you to bed," he said, "but it's too soon for that, isn't it?"

She didn't answer. She didn't have an answer. Her body was betraying her. Maybe she *could* steal a few days of pleasure. Except she'd never been able to do that. She'd been a virgin when she met her husband. And he'd been her only sexual partner. She wasn't a prude. It was just that since that betrayal and her own bad judgment, she hadn't cared enough about anyone to give away that part of her.

Not until now. She thought of the moment she'd first seen him. Relaxed. Sitting alone in the library near midnight with several days of beard and a stained T-shirt. Even then, her heart had accelerated.

His arms tightened around her. The hold was more gentle than lustful and yet she felt a certain tension in his body and knew it must be responding in the same way as her own. The heat that seared her everywhere their bodies touched must also burn him.

His lips came down slowly to meet hers, skimming more than pressing as if posing their own question. She reached up and touched his face, tracing its strong angles and then her arms went up around his neck and she stretched up on her toes.

Her body tingled in reaction to his. Tingled and ached. He leaned down and kissed her again, this time with exquisite tenderness.

Then he pulled away. "You should go," he said softly, "before we do something we both might regret."

She didn't want to go. Her body ached with need for him but he was right. It was madness. She stepped back.

Ross gave her a crooked grin as he released her. "You're not sure, and I want you to be sure," he said.

She looked up at him and nodded.

He touched her face again. "In the meantime," he added, "Hobo and I thank you again for all the help today."

"I don't think you needed any," she said.

"More than you know," he replied.

There was a strange note in his voice. But then he smiled again.

"I'll see you in the morning at the ranch," she said awkwardly. "Don't forget there's breakfast in the lobby and don't hesitate to call the front desk if you need anything." Why did her usual spiel sound so forced?

"I won't," he said. "Tell Vagabond I said hello."

"She'll be thrilled," Susan said with a sudden grin that broke some of the stiffness between them.

She left on that note, knowing that the image of a shirtless Ross Taylor standing in the door was not going to be that easy to banish. She'd had precious little sleep in the past two days. She doubted whether she would get much tonight.

Ross stared at the closed door for several seconds.

He liked her. A lot. Probably too much. She was an intriguing mixture of businesslike inn manager, sympathetic riding instructor and apparent friend to everyone—as well as being a very attractive woman with a sense of humor.

He didn't like games, and she didn't play any. What you saw was what you got. But he was definitely drawn to her, and she was not someone with whom he could have a mutually enjoyable fling. Something happened in Las Vegas. He'd watched her eyes cloud as she mentioned it. She'd been wounded and yet it didn't seem to affect her obvious desire to cure the world, or as much of it as she could.

Dammit, she touched him in ways no other woman did and, damn it, it happened so fast. He wanted her in the worst way but couldn't force himself to push any more than he had.

He swore as he gulped down his glass of wine and poured another. He would prefer a large swallow of bourbon but he would take whatever he could get at the moment.

Small, throaty noises interrupted his discussion with himself.

"Okay," Ross said. "Food. I get it. You're hungry. You don't think I noticed some people slipping snacks to you?" He was pleased, though, that Hobo was demonstrating some initiative. Damn, he was talking to a dog as if it were human.

He opened the bag Susan had given him. There were several cans of dog food, along with a can opener; two small bowls; a leash and a collar; as well as some dog treats.

He opened a can of food and served it to Hobo, then took him outside with one of Susan's little bags in his hand. By pure habit, he checked out the bike. All looked as it should.

After a hot shower, he wrapped a towel around his waist and went to the floor-to-ceiling window.

It was a great room with a good view. It directly faced the mountain, and the moon made its white cap glow.

He retraced the day. He'd enjoyed it far more than he'd thought he would. Once he managed those first steps into the stables, he'd been able to ward off memories. Maybe it was Susan's matter-of-fact efficiency, but perhaps these two weeks would be healing for himself as well as the vets.

Then he skipped to the present and wondered what Susan meant when she'd referred to "magic in the mountains."

Hobo batted his leg with his paw and tried to climb up. Ross reached down and pulled him into his lap. "Don't get any ideas," he warned the dog. "This is a temporary gig. For both of us."

He took the book that Jubal had given him and looked over Travis's suggestions for the program, then the profiles of each of the participants. Seven of the fourteen were married. Six were divorced. One was single. They ranged in age from twenty-four to thirty-eight.

It was well after 1:00 a.m. before he finished.

Unfortunately, his thoughts continually turned to Susan.

He counted all the reasons they shouldn't.

She embraced life. It was apparent in the inn and all its special touches. It was in her enthusiasm for the vet program. It was in the way everyone not only respected her but felt she was a member of their family.

He, on the other hand, always tried to be an observer. It had been essential as a medic and useful now.

He tried a few more arguments.

She was completely devoted to her life in Covenant Falls. He was completely devoted to his life on wheels.

He didn't believe in permanence. She obviously did.

He made all those arguments to himself and then told himself he was an idiot. He was only going to be here for a brief time.

To hell with it. He was imagining problems where there were none.

He would simply try to avoid her.

Did she say she would run with them in the morning? He really was in trouble.

Vagabond was not a happy cat.

She started complaining the moment Susan opened the door. The food bowl was empty. Neglect was obvious.

Susan apologized profusely but Vagabond stalked away, climbed up on a chair and glared. Susan wondered if Vagabond smelled dog on her.

She shook her head. Vagabond had transformed from feral cat to prima donna.

Susan hurried to fill the food bowl with high-end cat food and added a piece of chicken from the inn's kitchen. Vagabond was often the happy recipient of leftovers. Today, though, the cat was having none of it. She was in a snit and not easily placated.

Susan filled the water bowl, tried to stroke the cat, but Vagabond jumped down and haughtily stalked to the food bowl where she deigned to nibble.

"Watch it," Susan said, "there's a dog in waiting."

Unimpressed, Vagabond just swished her tail.

Susan shook her head. The cat had not yet forgiven her for bringing little Hobo inside.

She wasn't going to beg any longer. She went straight to her bathroom. The candle and book were still beside the tub where she'd left them when she was called the night before.

She couldn't stop thinking about Ross Taylor. He seemed to be a mass of contradictions.

He was a loner who really wasn't one. He apparently

lived alone, rode alone, worked for himself and liked it that way. And yet she'd notice the instant connection he had with Jubal and Clint and Josh's stepson, Nick, as well as the vets enrolled in the program.

He seemed easygoing and yet she'd sensed an intensity about him when they entered the barn today. He'd straightened his shoulders as one would do when encountering something unpleasant.

All in all, he was a conundrum. An attractive puzzle within a puzzle.

It was a puzzle she didn't need.

Only her mother's creative substitution for dammit could describe her frustration.

"Tarnation!" she said with such frustration that Vagabond jumped.

Chapter 9

Ross's internal clock woke him at a little after five. He glanced at the actual clock. He'd overslept by ten minutes.

He practically leaped out of bed. It wouldn't be a good beginning to challenge a group of veterans to a 6:00 a.m. run if he didn't show up.

He took a quick shower, then shaved.

Hobo came next. Ross fed the dog a can of food provided by the dog's fairy godmother and made a note to himself to reimburse her in some way. He hoped the dog could see the veterinarian today.

Hobo was getting around better, but Ross wanted a doctor to look at the leg before more damage was done.

There was another reason he was loath to admit. He had to find a good home for Hobo before the dog became too attached to him. Or, he admitted, he might get too attached to the dog. He tried to dismiss the thought that he might be nearing the too-late point.

He would call her at nine o'clock. He hoped she would be open then.

He took his running shorts from the saddlebags and pulled them on. He would buy an extra pair of jeans today and keep them at the ranch for riding. Unfortunately running clothes weren't very useful for riding, nor jeans for running.

Using the pillowcase and the pocketknife he always carried, he rigged a sling for Hobo. As a former field medic, he'd learned to improvise. Then he went out to the lobby with Hobo limping behind him. It was empty but coffee and cinnamon rolls were laid out on a counter.

He ate two rolls, took another one for Hobo and then gulped down two cups of coffee. He placed Hobo in the sling and started running. It was still dark but a thin gold line was visible on the horizon. It should be splendid in another twenty minutes.

The weather was perfect, and it felt great to be running again. It was his first good run in more than a week, and a daily run was a ritual with him. It was a good time to think, and this morning he had a lot to think about.

After seeing the hope and enthusiasm—along with some apprehension—among the veterans yesterday, he knew he was meant to be here. It was ironic his military service had only exacerbated his childhood trauma.

He hadn't believed in permanence since childhood. His army service and the pain and death he found there hadn't helped. His satisfaction now came from aiding the healing process, whether it was an elderly person with a broken hip or a veteran who had lost a leg.

This effort of Josh and Jubal—the two *J*s—to alleviate some of the emotional wounds of war would change lives. Josh had sent him the profiles of the participants who were in the program. They had been referred to New Beginnings by either the VA or a veterans' help organization.

He knew many came back to the States unfit and unprepared for existing jobs, and to friends and families that could never understand why they woke up screaming or drank too much to forget what they'd seen or couldn't go out of the house because a loud noise might paralyze them.

So here he was, ready to help, and his initial reluctance due to canceling his long-planned trip faded away yesterday when he saw the pride the vets already had in their horses. Josh hoped some would make a career in the equine field. There was still a need for cowboys and then there were instructors, trainers, grooms, carriage drivers and other equine-related jobs.

Other participants, it was hoped, would go home with tools to better cope with civilian life.

His thoughts turned to Susan as he neared the ranch. They were doing that all too frequently, which was ridiculous. He'd never known a woman with whom he'd felt so comfortable. Dammit, but he wanted to spend more time with her, and that was dangerous. Their lifestyles were a thousand miles apart, and he didn't intend to change his.

So why do you keep gravitating toward her?

Ross reached the road into the ranch. The sun was more visible now, layering the plain to the east in gold. He continued to run until he reached the bunkhouse. To his surprise all of the vets, including Kate, whom he had learned had been a former army truck driver, were waiting for him. It was a motley group, some in jeans, some in fatigue pants, some in shorts.

Susan was there with them, and a jolt of adrenaline rushed through him. She wore running shorts, along with a comfortable-looking T-shirt and a light jacket. Her hair was pulled back in one long braid.

She looked fresh and happy as she talked to several of the guys who hung on to every word. He went over to her side. "How's Vagabond?" he asked.

"Irritated," she said. "She's stalking around the house. I think she believes I'm consorting with the enemy."

He raised an eyebrow. "The enemy?"

"Hobo," she explained. "She apparently sniffed his scent on me. She doesn't care for dogs. Or cats. Or most people." She paused, then added, "I like the sling. You'll have to show me how you did that."

Before he could answer, she reached inside and plucked Hobo out of the sling. The dog protested and wriggled to get back to Ross.

"What am I'm going to do with him now?" he said. "I can't keep him in the sling."

"I have news for you. I called Stephanie last night after she got back. She'll see Hobo at noon."

"That's great. I was going to call when she opened this morning. Thanks."

Scott, one of the vets he'd met last night, piped up. "I'll make a bed for him in the bathroom," he said.

Ross looked at Susan. She nodded. "He'll be safe, and we won't be gone long."

He nodded. "Hobo has to learn to be more independent." He tried to dismiss the dog's anxious grunt as Susan handed the pup to Scott. Hobo tried to wriggle out of his hands and the grunt turned into a frantic bark.

Ross almost grabbed the dog back, but that would only make Hobo more reliant on him.

"Looks like you're stuck with him," Susan said. "He prefers to be jostled than left behind."

She wasn't being helpful. "He'll be okay," he said, hoping it was true. "Hobo will discover there are good people in this world."

He tried to erase the image of the dog from his mind and concentrate on the run ahead as Scott and Hobo disappeared into the bunkhouse. "I think one mile is enough for today," he said to the group. "We'll add more as we go along." He turned to Susan. "Which way?" he asked.

"Turn east when we reach the road. It just goes to a few ranches. There's very little traffic. Probably none at this time."

"East it is," he said. He waited until Scott rejoined them, then started at a slow jog. He held back a little until everyone was on the road. After a few minutes, he noticed that Susan fell back. By design, he suspected. She would go to the rear, take care of any stragglers. He had gotten to know her in the past hours. She was the ultimate caretaker. Part of the glue that held the town and community together.

It was scary as hell that he was attracted to her.

He increased the pace. He nodded to the veteran next to him, who was matching him stride for stride.

After they ran half a mile, he turned around. Despite the fact that during their service years they probably ran ten miles without a problem, more than a few were obviously struggling. Despite the cool air, most were sweating as they returned to the bunkhouse.

"Want some coffee, sir?" one of the vets said. His name was Jake and he was from Oklahoma.

"I'm not 'sir,'" Ross said. "Just call me Ross like you call Luke Daniels Luke and Jubal Pierce Jubal. Tell the others, okay? And I *would* like coffee."

"I'll get you one."

"Thanks. But I'd better learn where it is. I drink too much of it."

"I'll show you." Jake led the way inside to the kitchen area. There was a carafe of coffee on a hot plate and a pile of coffee cups. Ross filled one up and ignored the sugar and cream.

"Thanks," he said. "I remember you from last night. You have a good voice."

"Thanks, but Clint is the greatest."

"I have to agree with that but you're no slouch."

Just then he heard loud barking from another room.

"Excuse me," he said, and headed toward the washroom and opened the door. Hobo was behind one of the commodes even as he barked. Ross picked him up. Hobo was shaking. Ross wished he knew what had happened to him before they'd met. He recalled the scars he'd seen while bathing him. "It's okay," he said. "No one will hurt you."

He sighed. He couldn't carry him everywhere. Hobo was just going to have to learn that he was safe, that not everyone wanted to hurt him.

Ross fastened the new leash on Hobo, then took his coffee out to where several men stood. "I think my first appointment this morning is Riley." He looked at the exhausted group.

A lanky man raised his hand.

"Why don't you get some coffee," Ross said, "and we'll grab some chairs outside. When is your riding session?"

"It's at ten, sir. I mean, Ross."

"Do you mind the dog joining us?"

"No…he's good."

"He's great with confidentiality," Ross said with a grin. "Go ahead and get some coffee while I stake out some chairs.

Minutes later Riley was back with coffee. Ross started by asking him about his service.

"I spent four years in Afghanistan," Riley said.

"Then you saw combat?"

"Yeah. My best buddy was killed by an Afghan soldier who was supposed to be on our side. George was standing next to me. I was wounded. We'd been shot at before. You couldn't trust anybody…"

"And you still can't?" He didn't use notes. They tended to put people off, and now it was just a matter of getting to know them, why they'd come here and what they expected to accomplish.

"I guess so."

"Why did you sign up for the program?"

"I don't know," he said. "Meant to stay in the army and put in my twenty years, but after George was killed I couldn't do that. I kept seeing George's chest…explode. My tour was up. I thought if I got away from the army, I wouldn't see it.

"Didn't work," Riley continued. "Kept having flashbacks. I started drinking. My wife left me. She got real tired of me waking her up with a yell. I couldn't get interested in anything. Kept quitting nowhere jobs. A buddy from the army told me about New Beginnings. He was in the first group. It helped him get his head on straight."

"Ever ridden a horse before?"

"Nope. I was a city kid."

"Work out at a gym or at home in the past few years?"

"No. Didn't seem any point in it."

"You said you were injured. Anything I should know about that might affect different forms of exercise?" Ross asked.

"I was hit in the thigh. Had some pins put in, but it doesn't give me any trouble."

"Good. I'm glad you joined us this morning."

"I almost didn't," Riley said ruefully.

"But you did and that's what is important." Ross wasn't a psychologist and didn't want to pretend to be one. But he thought it was important to know the motivation for coming here.

"How do you like your horse?" he said, changing the subject.

"He's good," Riley said but Ross detected a lack of enthusiasm. "But I'm not very good riding him. I feel like a sack of potatoes holding on for dear life."

"Not for long, I expect."

"I mean, some people can sing. Some can draw. Some can ride horses. What if I'm not one of the latter?"

"Then I might be in trouble, too," Ross said. "I'm not very graceful on a horse, either."

"Can I ask you something?" Riley said.

"Sure."

"Were you in combat?"

"Yes, same place as you, but I was a medic. I was in Iraq, too."

"Did you ever have PTSD?"

Ross nodded.

"Did…you get over it?"

Ross considered the question. "No," he said honestly. "But I can control it better." He paused, then added, "Exercise helps. Work until you fall in bed. Find something you love doing, even if it takes years to accomplish it."

He remembered something from the notes he'd been given. It mentioned a woman who trained homeless dogs for vets with severe PTSD. He would ask Travis about it. It might help Riley.

"I'll be hanging around this evening," he said. "I have an appointment at seven with someone, but we'll talk about some exercises."

Susan smiled as she watched Ross and Riley Conway pick up two camp chairs and carry them to a spot under a big tree. Hobo hobbled behind Ross on the leash she'd bought. She heard little grunting noises. She surmised it was Hobo's vocal version of happy. The two men sat down and Hobo huddled as close to Ross as possible.

Stop it, she told herself. It was stupid to care. She turned her attention to the remaining vets. They were kidding each other, proud that they had made a mile this morning. Several went inside, probably to change clothes and eat breakfast. She knew they were on their own for both breakfast and lunch, and the kitchen was fully stocked.

She walked over to the barn. Danny had brought the horses in from the paddocks at daybreak and she wanted to say hello to them. She knew most of them, had ridden several.

One man was sitting on a bale of hay. She recognized him, having met him last night at the party. Simon Moore. He'd been the last to return from the run and was the least responsive of the guests. One of the other guys said he was forced into the program by his wife, who'd threatened to leave him if he didn't get help.

"Hi," she said. "I was glad to see you on the run."

"I didn't do so well."

"But you pushed yourself. That's a good start. Wait until six weeks are over."

He looked dubious.

"You're riding Sara. She's a sweetheart."

He nodded without enthusiasm.

"Want some help in feeding her?"

"She doesn't like me!" he complained.

"How do you know?"

"She showed me her teeth."

"Did you give her a carrot?"

"No."

"I think she might be asking for one."

"You think?"

"Why don't you try it? There's a bucketful at the front."

He disappeared and returned with a carrot. And hesitated.

She wondered how he had avoided this first step. He should have been taught all this by now. "Just offer it. She won't bite."

Simon tentatively held the carrot and Sara scoffed it down and looked expectant. He blinked, not sure whether this was a good thing.

"Did you saddle Sara yesterday?"

"I didn't feel well."

She was right. He didn't want to be here. He was probably afraid of horses but apparently his wife forced his hand. He was clever enough to get someone else to help him saddle the first time and then probably made an excuse to hang back.

"She's very gentle," she said. "She's like a rocking

horse, and she loves anyone who gives her carrots and feeds her. Let's get some oats and put them in her feed bucket. You will have a friend for life."

Simon looked at her with frank disbelief.

She took the bucket from the stall and showed him where the feed was and how much to give Sara. He followed instructions and Sara nuzzled his hand.

"It's soft," he said, looking surprised.

"When are you supposed to have your first riding session?" she asked.

"This afternoon."

"Is it okay if I give you some pointers?"

Several of the other men came in and started feeding and watering their horses. She saw his shoulders get a little straighter.

Thirty minutes later he was riding in one of the riding rings. Stiff at first. Fingers clutching the saddle horn, then gradually loosening. After another half hour, he started to relax. He walked around the circle several more times.

"Ready for breakfast now?" she asked.

She went over and held the horse. "Just swing your right leg over and slide down. Then walk him back to the barn, unsaddle him and cool him down. Okay? You can show up the instructor this afternoon now."

He gave her what she thought must be a rare smile. "Thanks," he said. "Yeah, I can do it." He and Sara headed for the barn.

Susan turned around and saw Ross standing next to a tree. "Nice work," he said. "From what I read and heard, I thought we might lose him."

She noticed it was *we*. "How did you know I was here?" she asked.

"One of the guys saw you lead him here. He was a

little worried. Simon made no secret about not wanting to be here."

"He was more afraid than anything. I suspect there was an unfortunate encounter with a horse somewhere in his past."

Something flickered in Ross's eyes. But it was gone almost immediately.

"You should be an instructor," Ross said.

"I've worked with some kids," she said, "but I would rather just ride. Like your bike, it's my freedom."

"I get that," he said.

"I thought you would." Their gazes met. She tried to look away but something held her. His eyes showed little about what he was thinking. It amazed her that he could manage that. She always jumped into every cause with fervor.

Problem now was she should be running in the other direction.

Still, words popped out of her mouth.

"Need a lift to Stephanie's office?"

He hesitated, then nodded. "I need to buy some clothes, as well."

"Then you'will need a ride. I don't think running will work. You don't have enough hands for clothes and a dog." She was asking for trouble but she couldn't help herself. "You can even drive," she taunted, "*if* you can drive a four-wheel vehicle?"

"When I must," he said with a lopsided grin that made her heart turn over. She winced. Why in the heck was she asking for trouble? She didn't want her heart to turn over. It was the worst thing that could possibly happen.

"I'll be in the stables helping anyone who needs it," she said. "I'll find you at eleven thirty." She turned around and walked toward the stable. It had been a dumb offer. He was perfectly capable of getting his own ride from someone at the ranch.

She could only hope that he would say or do something that would spoil her opinion of him. Unfortunately it was the opposite. Physical therapist for the stars or not, he cared about *her* vets. It had been obvious last night and again this morning.

And they responded to him. He connected to them in a way she never could because he'd shared some of their experiences. His understanding was unspoken but demonstrated in the respect he gave them.

She hadn't noticed any physical wounds but she would bet he had emotional ones. She knew medics often had the worst of it. They were right there in the action and charged with doing all they could to save bodies torn apart by explosions and bullets and often there was little they could do.

How did he go from that to working with film stars? Why didn't he work for the VA or with other programs where physical therapy improved lives, instead of helping careers?

And why did he insist on a nomadic lifestyle?

Two big questions she'd love to have answered.

Chapter 10

Along with Danny, Susan spent the rest of the morning helping the vets care for their horses and gear. They fed their horses, talked to them, saddled and unsaddled them during the course of the morning.

She made sure the girths were tight and the stirrups adjusted properly, that they cooled off the horses on return to the stable. It was the participants' second day on horseback. They were feeling more at ease.

She loved doing it. She already saw changes in their guests. They were less nervous, less uptight in just these two days. They complained of sore butts—"beg your pardon, miss."

When the stable cleared out, she walked out to the riding ring. Four vets were being asked for a slow canter while Luke watched and shouted instructions. She knew Luke had already decided their skill levels, or lack of them, and divided the participants into three categories: stark beginners, some experience and good riders. Luke worked with the beginning riders and Jubal and Josh with the middle group. After basic skills were developed, the the vets would graduate into advanced horsemanship, including herding cattle and teaching horsemanship themselves.

She checked her watch. Eleven thirty. Time for them to leave for Stephanie's animal clinic. She hadn't seen Ross since they'd talked earlier. Temporarily at loose ends, she tried the bunkhouse. Ross was on the floor with Dennis, one of the quietest of the group. They were doing push-ups. Both were sweating. Hobo was lying a few feet away, his eyes on Ross.

"That's enough," he said to Dennis. "Unless you want to keep going."

"No, sir." Relief was evident in his voice.

Ross raised an eyebrow.

"I mean Mr. Taylor. Ah… Ross."

"Got it right the last time. Keep going with those push-ups in the morning," he said. "See if you can work up to twenty. How did the riding lesson go this morning?"

"Better than yesterday but I'm sore as hell today." Then Dennis noted her standing at the door. "Beg your pardon, ma'am, I mean…" he stuttered.

"Don't mind me," she said. "I've used that expression several times."

Dennis stared at her. "You have?"

"Afraid so," she said, then changed the subject. "Have you been on a horse before?"

"Just an old farm mule."

"That counts," she said.

"How did you hear about New Beginnings?" Ross broke in.

"The VA. A counselor there. He suggested that I come here. I couldn't hold a job. Every loud noise freaked me out. Couldn't sleep. Started drinking too much. Trying to forget things I saw."

The young man cut his gaze at her. "I still want a drink," he said, "but Ross, he told me whenever I thought about taking a drink, I should start doing push-ups until I was too tired to want one anymore."

"Sounds good to me," she said.

"There isn't anything around to test the theory," he said with a shy smile.

Susan nodded. "But push-ups do sound like a good idea. I might try that."

"Can't do them like I used to," Dennis added regretfully. "Got to get my body back in shape for the camping trip. Ross said he would work with me on that."

Ross rose in one graceful movement, leaned down and pulled Dennis up.

She noticed both men's T-shirts were damp with sweat. She wondered how long they had been at this.

Ross looked at his watch. "I need a quick shower. Do we have time before the veterinarian appointment?"

"Stephanie won't care if we're a few minutes late. I think she would prefer you have a shower."

He gave her that slow smile that caused heart fluctuations. "I'll just be five minutes."

She noticed Hobo was starting after him. She swooped down and picked him up. "You can trust me," she told the dog. "He'll be right back."

She made small talk with Dennis, and several minutes later, Jubal entered the bunkhouse with a shirt in his hands. "Ross called. Said he needed a clean shirt."

"He's washing up."

Jubal went straight to the shower room.

Jubal and Ross came out together. Ross was wearing a blue pullover shirt that was a little snug. It outlined every muscle and the color looked great with his gray eyes. "Let's go," he said.

"Have you had anything to eat?" she asked Ross.

"Not yet. I was going to grab a sandwich here."

"Can you take more time in town?"

He nodded. "Next meeting here isn't until two."

"That will do," she said. "You haven't been to Maude's. Best diner in Colorado and a veteran's first visit is free. After you see Stephanie, you can visit the General Store while I check in at the inn and then we can meet at Maude's for lunch. You can leave Hobo with Stephanie while we eat or you can take her to Maude's. She doesn't notice if you sneak in a dog. No food inspectors around here. Amos is a well-known figure there."

"She sneaks dogs in?" he asked.

She noticed he didn't jump at the chance to leave Hobo with the vet. "No, she just makes a point of not noticing. She's much too busy."

His grin widened. "Okay. I want to get clothes to keep some at the ranch. Running to work has disadvantages."

"The General Store manager is very nimble in her buying," Susan said. "If she doesn't have what you need, she'd have it tomorrow even if she has to drive to Pueblo to get it."

"I'm beginning to like this town," Ross replied. "Free meals. Accommodating stores."

"That's the idea," she said.

"I know," he said. "'We aim to please,'" he said, repeating one of her earlier statements. He turned to Dennis. "Good job today. That wasn't easy, and I know it. I'm proud of you."

She watched as Dennis seemed to grow another inch or two taller as he straightened up. "Thanks."

"Same time tomorrow," Ross told him. "And I would take a long hot shower to relieve some of those sore muscles."

"I think there will be a line tonight," Dennis said shyly.

"I expect there will," Ross said, then turned to Susan. "Let's go." He leaned down and picked up Hobo, who had been restrained for the time Ross was in the shower room. "I'm going to tell Luke I'm leaving," he added. "Can you take Hobo? He accepts you. I'll meet you at the car."

She leaned down and picked up Hobo. The leash she'd bought wasn't necessary. He didn't need one. It was clear he wasn't going far from Ross.

A few other vets were still in the ring with Luke. She knew it was all very organized and that in the next few weeks the groups would meld together into one competent group of riders when they took the wilderness trip. There would be other rides together, as well. They would have new confidence, new abilities, new coping skills.

She was impressed but not surprised at the way Ross melded so easily into the program. And she was beginning to understand how he became a physical therapist for film stars. He had patience, empathy and a way of becoming a partner rather than an instructor. He was also the kind of man she suspected film stars would respect:

a former Ranger with combat experience and a body any star would probably die for.

It was difficult to put that together with the kind of outsider—or wanderer—he seemed determined to be. Given a choice, how could someone not have a home? Not have any roots? Nor want any?

Before she could muse any longer, he was at the Jeep. His hair was still damp and the fresh shirt stuck to him. She was hard put not to stare.

When they reached Stephanie's office, Susan entered with Ross and Hobo and introduced them.

Stephanie studied Ross as she held out her hand. "I'm sorry I missed you the last couple days."

"I heard you were on a search and rescue mission. Was it successful?"

"Depends on the way you look at it. A woman took a wrong turn and ran out of gas. No cell service. She left the car and started walking. She was in the mountains and fell. She has multiple injuries. We finally found her thanks to some good guesses by very smart forest rangers and one of my search dogs, but it's going to be a miracle if she gets back to where she was physically. One hint," she added. "If you ever get lost, stay in or around your car. More people die from wandering off." Then she looked at Hobo. "I take it this is my newest patient."

Ross nodded. "He's obviously had a hard time. I found him shot and left on a mountain road. His leg looked bad. I did what I could with a makeshift splint. He's walking, but I know animals can stand a great deal of pain. As you can tell, he's obviously been mistreated for a long time. When I found him he was filthy."

Stephanie picked Hobo up. "I'll run a series of blood

tests and check that leg." She rubbed the dog's tummy. Hobo moaned. There were no other words for that.

"That's pleasure, not pain," Stephanie explained.

"He has a lot of scars," Ross inserted. "I think maybe he was a bait dog for a dog fighting ring. He's not large enough or strong enough to actually fight."

Susan bit her lip. If true, it was a miracle Hobo had survived. No wonder he feared everyone but the man who had saved him. Her affection for the little dog spiraled upward.

Susan broke in. "I'll leave the two of you. I should check in at the inn." She turned to Ross. "I'll meet you at Maude's. If you get there first, just tell her you're with me, although she probably knows all about you now."

Stephanie smiled. "She's right about that. It's scary."

Susan left and drove to the inn a mile away. The parking lot looked ghostly with only a few cars parked, several of them belonging to staff. It would fill up Friday and Saturday nights when the dining room offered dinners that drew ranchers from miles around, as well as townspeople.

It was a regular feature and helped keep the inn solvent when room bookings slacked off.

But today, she had bills to pay and orders to make. She also wanted to check comments on the inn that had been submitted by recent guests. To her satisfaction, there were five from last week's guests on the inn's website. All recommended the pageant, two mentioned the gold mine Jeep trip. The inn itself received five stars on four of the comments and four on the fifth.

She copied them for possible marketing value, then glanced at the clock. It was one fifteen. She was running a little late. She pulled in front of Maude's four minutes later. The great thing about small towns was short distances and light traffic.

Susan saw Ross immediately when she opened the door to Maude's. Maude had seated him at her favorite table, the corner booth next to the window. She was a sucker for veterans.

Maude scurried over to her. "He's a good one," she said.

"How do you know?" Susan asked.

"His smile. I can always tell by their smile."

"Josh didn't smile the first time he came here," Susan reminded her.

"Ah…but I could tell under all that gruffness was a big heart."

"You just plain like everyone," Susan charged. "Admit it."

"Not quite everyone," Maude said. "I have several on my watch list."

"Who?"

"That's for me to know," she said, and led the way through the packed restaurant to the back booth.

"Hi," Susan said as she slid into the seat facing Ross. "What did Stephanie say?"

"The wound is healing nicely. No parasites, which is a miracle. He's getting a more professional splint. The leg was broken but she thinks it's already healing. He's a tough little guy. That's about it."

"Where is he now?"

"He's still there but we have to pick him up. She thought it would be better if he stayed with me while she checked around for possible adopters."

"You didn't disagree."

He looked shamefaced. "I couldn't leave him in one

of those small cages. Not after everything he's gone through. But she said she would try to find a real home for him."

Ross didn't sound as eager about the prospect of finding a home for Hobo as he had yesterday. And she very much doubted Stephanie would look very hard. She knew a good match when she saw one. Susan smiled inside. Or maybe it wasn't so internal because he cast her a suspicious look. "No," he said. "I really can't keep him."

Maude interrupted them then. "What can I get you?"

He glanced up at her. "What would you suggest?

"The T-bone today," she said. "Comes with salad and French fries. Best yet, it's free."

"That's an offer I can't refuse."

Maude studied him for a moment. "My goodness, but you look like you need a really big steak. And I bet you like it rare."

"Yes, ma'am," he said. "To both."

Maude smiled. "What about you, Susan?"

"A filet and salad. He's a lot bigger than I am."

Maude nodded. "He is that. I'll have it in fifteen minutes. Welcome to Covenant Falls, Mr. Taylor."

He raised an eyebrow. "How did you know…?"

"Tell him, Susan," Maude said, and hurried away with the order.

"Maude knows everything that happens in Covenant Falls and sometimes before it happens," she explained. "Everyone eats here and everyone confides in her. She has a special affection for the military. Her husband was killed in Desert Storm. The town became her family."

"How many stories are there in Covenant Falls?" he asked.

"As many as there are people and then some."

"What about yours?" he said. "Why do you stay when there's such big world out there?"

She shrugged. "Why do you not have any home at all?"

"Touché," he said.

"That's not a good answer. I've never known anyone who didn't have some place they called home, humble or princely."

He shrugged. "I have a job that keeps me on the road."

"You could work anywhere," she said. "Physical therapists are in demand."

He raised an eyebrow. "They are?"

"That's what I read." She realized then that she had given away her interest. She was mortified.

Maude suddenly appeared with two iced teas. Susan took a long swallow, then met Ross's gaze after Maude left. Since she had already let it be known that she'd probably done some research, she pursued the topic. "I also read that you worked with some Hollywood stars."

"Did it mention any names?"

"Just one. A photographer caught you leaving his house."

Ross nodded. "He wasn't happy about that."

She had a lot of questions, but looking at his cool gray eyes, she thought those questions could wait for another day.

"Did you go by the General Store?"

"Yeah. I have to admit I was happily surprised." He paused, then asked, "That really is the proper name? Not Clancy's Superstore, or Mary's Emporium?"

"We're not fancy in Covenant Falls. We call things as they are," she explained.

"Just the facts, ma'am?"

"Something like that. Did it meet your standards?"

"I don't have many," he said. "But if I did, it would. It surpassed them. You should see the pile next to me. Two T-shirts, a pair of wrinkle-free slacks and a shirt. Even a pair of riding boots. I'll leave them at the ranch." He paused, then added, "That's actually a shopping spree for me."

"I can see that," she said with a grin. "Is that what you wear for your other clients?"

"Josh isn't a client," he said. "But yes, it usually is. They don't employ me for my wardrobe."

"Why do they? Employ you, I mean?"

"I'm good at it. I'm discreet and I don't lie to them," he said matter-of-factly. "I tell them in the beginning what I can and can't do, and the former depends on how hard they work."

"How did you get started?"

He shrugged. "The traveling part? I knew I didn't want a full-time job with a rehab center or hospital. I'm not crazy about staying anywhere long. I was older than the other students and grew close to one of my professors. We had talks, and he knew I was restless. I almost dropped out at one point. He suggested going the per diem route, and when I graduated he recommended me to an agency in Hollywood."

He shrugged. "A lot of their clientele were stars and stuntmen. I understand their world and how crucial time is to them. They want the fastest rehab possible without incurring more damage. I tell them like it is. But though it pays most of the bills, it's a minor part of my business, time-wise. I do other jobs as well, including stints at VA and other rehab facilities that have temporary gaps. I've worked with private individuals for various reasons. The main advantage of being a traveling therapist is the ability to choose."

"And what do you think about New Beginnings?"

"I like it. I like the emphasis on vets helping each other. It's what they missed since leaving the service. Hopefully, they will keep in touch after the six weeks and become a continuing support group. I particularly appreciate the fact that they'll be welcomed back anytime they feel a need for it.

"The greatest cause of suicides and drug addiction among veterans," he added with an intensity that surprised her, "is isolation, the feeling that no one understands what they experienced: the fear, the injuries, the loss of buddies, the guilt for surviving when others didn't.

"Six weeks won't solve that," he added, "but friendships and new tools to face those problems will help.

"Sorry to get on my soapbox," he added with a wry smile. "You know all that. But what impresses me most is the way the entire community is supporting it."

"It comes naturally. Covenant Falls has always been military oriented. It's given more than its share to the military and its casualty lists throughout its one-hundred-and-fifty-year history. You probably haven't seen it yet, but there's a military memorial in the park adjacent to the lake."

"I'll have to visit it." He hesitated, then started slowly, "There's one veteran—Riley..."

"I know him," she said. "He's...withdrawn."

"He's afraid he can't ever ride. Maybe he needs some of your magic."

"I'll try to run into him tomorrow at the barn," she replied.

The steaks came then, and conversation stopped.

* * *

It was 9:00 p.m. before Ross finished with the evening group meeting. He told them a little about his background. It helped that he'd been an army medic for three tours before getting his degree. He'd already had private sessions with five of the fourteen participants and arranged more with the others over the next two days.

In the general meeting, he discussed and demonstrated exercises that would improve their balance and strengthen muscles helpful in riding, along with others that would be beneficial in everyday living.

"Some of you—probably all—will be sore for several more days but then the aches will fade away." He made it clear that he was available at any time and asked for their input as to what they felt they needed, wanted and didn't want.

"What about doing away with push-ups," one quipped.

"Good try," he said. "Did I add that I might not follow subtle hints?" Everyone laughed.

"But seriously," he added, "this is not a jail or the army. Certain exercises will help you become better riders. Others will help you become healthier people. But no one, including me, will be taking notes or keeping track of whether you do or don't."

He finished by thanking them for their cooperation and participation in the session. "I'm here for questions, advice, as a complaint board or whatever you need. I'll be riding and learning with you, and I'll have the same aches and pain and probably tumbles.

"Which reminds me," he said with a grin, "After this morning's stellar performance, I'll be leading an optional run each morning at six." He wanted them to take responsibility, not just to be told what to do. He planned to give each vet a suggested voluntary action plan depending on their physical condition. He hoped peer competition would drive them.

He left the bunkhouse with Hobo, who'd stayed next to him. The dog had allowed other vets to touch him as long as Ross was within huddling distance. By the end of the evening, every vet was arguing about who was more successful.

Ross walked outside. He didn't see Susan or her car and assumed she'd left earlier. He tamped down unexpected disappointment. She had a job and a life. She couldn't spend all her time babysitting him.

He was resigned to running or—more likely—walking to the inn with Hobo in the sling when Jubal appeared. "I'll give you a ride back to the inn," he said. "Looks like we might have a storm coming."

"I can walk."

"Hell, it will take me less than ten minutes round trip," he said. "It's the least I can do."

"Then I accept. I didn't want to ride my bike over here. I was afraid it might spook the horses."

"You don't have to worry about that. They're well trained. They're used to the sound of heavy trucks and horse trailers."

"Good. It will be a lot more convenient."

"What about the little fellow?"

"He fits into a basket I made for the bike. He doesn't seem to mind."

"He sure sticks close to you."

"That's why I need to find a home for him as quickly as possible," Ross said. "What about you and your wife? Hobo needs a family."

"Not unless I want to get hit by a flying frying pan.

Right now Lisa has a medical practice, two sibling teenagers, their dog, three employees and a continuous flow of veterans with various stages of PTSD."

"Maybe he'd make a good watchdog?" Desperation prodded him to keep talking.

"That little guy? He would make a burglar laugh."

"That's one way of disarming him," Ross shot back.

"Why do you assume the burglar is a him?" Jubal asked.

"Okay, one way of disarming *her*."

Jubal chuckled. "Sorry, but no help here. By the way, you seem to be getting along with Susan."

"She's hard not to like," Ross replied.

"That is true," Jubal said as they reached what looked like a well-used minivan. "None of my business anyway."

"A minivan?" Ross asked with a raised eyebrow as he eyed the vehicle with something akin to horror.

"It happens when you gain a family and a ranch," Jubal said with a sheepish smile.

"Where are the kids?"

"Gordon is at college, studying aeronautic engineering. He can design anything," he added proudly. "Kerry's a high school junior and a good little horsewoman. This first weekend of the vet program is always hectic, and she has tests next week. She's staying with a friend studying this weekend."

Jubal sounded completely domesticated. It was darn right scary to see two warriors like Jubal and Josh so tamed. Ross silently swore it wasn't going to happen to him. He was a wandering man. Free from any ties. He cherished the freedom of his lifestyle.

They were turning into the inn when a streak of lightning crossed the sky. Ross said a quick good-night. He wanted to cover the bike if he was going to ride it in the morning.

"See you in the morning?" Jubal said.

"Yeah. Want to go running with us—6:00 a.m.? I know I didn't think it wise the first time, but now I want them to become a little competitive."

"Sure, why not," Jubal said. "I've been so busy with the ranch, haven't done much of it lately."

Ross went in the side door to his room and put Hobo down, then returned to the bike and covered it. He stayed there for a moment, enjoying the wind that was now blowing strong.

Then he went inside.

He took out his cell, did some searching, then punched in his order and credit card information. His order was immediately confirmed, and the item should arrive in two days.

When he put the cell down, he made a bet with himself on the morning run. Then, exhausted, he went to bed.

Chapter 11

Ross woke to the sound of thunder and the softer sound of scratching at the side of the bed.

It took him a minute to recognize it.

Hobo was frantically trying to get up on the bed.

Lightning flashed into the room and he understood Hobo's terror. How many times had the dog tried to find shelter?

Ross hated storms, as well.

Too often it brought back the scene from the farm. The thunder that woke him up, the neighing of alarmed horses that sensed something was terribly wrong...

He never knew why his father chose that method of death, why he'd left his only child or his wife to find him. *I've never forgiven you for that.*

Ross looked at the clock. It was a little after 3:00 a.m. He lifted Hobo up on the bed. The dog was trembling with fear.

He remembered the dog he had as a boy. Patches loved having his stomach rubbed. Ross turned Hobo around and started rubbing the dog's stomach. A kind of purring from deep in Hobo's throat touched him as few other things had in recent years. The dog had been so helpless, thrown away for reasons he couldn't understand.

Like Ross had been.

He knew the reasons years later, but it never erased the memories of a kid who'd lost all he loved in a matter of days. His family. His home. His horse. His dog.

And now he was relating to this dog in a way that meant trouble. He knew he wouldn't go back to sleep now. The freshly revived images would stay with him for days.

"Hey," he said to Hobo when the thunder faded away. "Need to go outside?"

He didn't wait for an answer. He rolled out of bed and reached for the running shorts he'd left in a chair near his bed. He pulled on his T-shirt, then his shoes.

He plucked Hobo, along with the new leash, and went outside. The storm had apparently rolled on. Water still dripped from trees and from the roof. Hobo looked up at him as if wondering, *What now?*

"Damn if I know," he said. He only knew that he was restless. He wouldn't sleep now. His mind was too jumbled from the nightmare. *Don't think about the past. Think about now.*

He reviewed yesterday. On the whole, it had been successful. Any concerns he had about the program had been alleviated. It was well researched and apparently well executed.

He should have known. Josh wouldn't have been connected with anything haphazard. From the notes he'd read, the vets—guests—were well chosen. The volunteers were knowledgeable and conscientious. Everyone connected to the program appeared to be competent and receptive to suggestions.

His only concern was Susan. He couldn't remember when he'd ever felt so connected to a woman in so short a time.

He liked her sense of humor, her commitment to the project and the guests, her general competence. Most of all he liked her open smile that included everyone she encountered. He hadn't missed the protective affection that both Josh and Jubal displayed toward her. She must have flaws but he hadn't noticed any yet except, maybe, her clear determination that he keep Hobo. Maybe her heart was *too* big.

He'd missed seeing her last night. Had she purposely avoided him or was there some emergency? And why did he care? Dammit, he did.

He took Hobo back inside. It was ten after four, but he knew he wouldn't sleep again.

He picked up the paperback—a mystery—he'd found at a truck stop several days ago and tried to read.

Susan woke up earlier than usual with a cat walking over her. She opened her eyes to the unblinking gaze of Vagabond staring at her. The cat obviously felt neglected and didn't waste time in telling Susan about it.

Susan had not reached her house until seven last night. She knew Ross was holding several sessions with the vets and would be occupied until late. There had been no reason to wait and drive him home despite her urge to do exactly that.

Hanging around was ridiculous and would indicate

an interest she didn't have. She had no doubt he could take care of himself in any situation and he certainly had friends. She understood he'd never met Jubal before he arrived and yet they talked as if they'd known each other forever.

Maybe it was just the warrior breed.

Whatever it was, she needed to stay away. She'd never been drawn to anyone like this before.

Not even Richard, her former husband. He had been as far from her small town life as he could be. Maybe that had been the attraction. Unlike Ross in his jeans and T-shirt and bike, Richard looked as if he'd stepped off a sophisticated magazine cover. He always dressed well, was always well groomed and hated it when she wasn't the same…

On her way home, she'd stopped at the inn. Mark was at the desk. All was well. Good, in fact, with four new drop-in guests and reservations for future dates."

"How is the vet program doing?" Mark asked.

"Even better than the last one." Susan added, "You're going a great job. I hope you know how much we appreciate you for filling in for me and all the extra hours."

He went red. "I'm grateful for the extra money and it's usually so quiet, I can study."

"Can you make sure we have coffee and pastries by five thirty? I expect we will have at least one large and hungry guest at that time."

"I know who you mean. Will do."

She headed home, only to hear complaints from Vagabond when she arrived.

"Sorry, girl," she said. "Promise to do better tomorrow."

She fed Vagabond, cleaned her litter box and took a

long hot bath. She had planned to read in the tub, but her mind was too busy. Instead she just luxuriated in the warm water. She'd helped out at New Beginnings because they needed it during the first few days. By tomorrow, most of the guests would know how to saddle, mount, dismount, cool off the horses and take care of the equipment. She wouldn't be needed.

She would spend tomorrow at the inn, doing what she was paid to do. Update the ad in the state tourism magazine. Send thank-you notes to recent guests and offer a discount for a repeat visit or to someone they recommended. She also intended to write a feature about the Jeep trip—which was apparently a real selling point—and peddle it to local papers in the area and travel magazines.

She'd been delinquent in those areas. She'd been sidetracked by one Ross Taylor, who'd made it clear he was a loner and never stayed in one place longer than a few weeks. Despite the attraction that flared between them, their lives were incompatible and it was foolish to let it go any further.

Goal for the next few days: avoid him.

Ross woke at five, debated about his transportation to the ranch. He could run, but Jubal said he could ride the bike and that would be a lot more convenient.

He had to wear jeans with the bike. He put the running shorts in his saddle bags along with his running shoes. He dropped by the lobby with hopes for fresh coffee and found it ready along with a plateful of pastries sitting on the counter.

He took a bite. They were good. Better than good. More like terrific. Warning himself he may not get into either jeans or shorts by the end of two weeks, he ate three large pastries. He fed Hobo and took him outside to do his business before tucking him into the basket on his bike. No protest. Hobo was obviously adaptable.

When he arrived, the vets were all outside, milling about in an assortment of clothing: jeans, cutoff jeans and shorts. Some of them were stretching. Some had coffee in their hands. Others were obviously trying to work out the soreness from yesterday's rides.

Neither Susan nor her car was visible. He didn't like the sudden jab of disappointment he felt. He'd looked forward to the spontaneous wide smile and some quip.

But it was 6:00 a.m. and his vets had a long day ahead of them. He quickly changed to running shorts and shoes and met them outside. Danny appeared and offered to take care of Hobo.

Then they were off. Jubal appeared from the barn, caught up with him and met his pace stride by stride. "Don't know why I didn't think of this," he said. "Great way to build unity as well as improve muscle strength." He looked around. "Susan not here today?"

"Doesn't look like it," Ross said. "She didn't mention it yesterday."

"Probably trying to catch up at the inn," Jubal said. "She's determined to make it successful."

"How did she get involved in it?" Ross asked.

"Her background is in the hospitality field. She was in management for several hotels before coming back here."

"Why did she come back?"

Jubal shrugged. "You'll have to ask her. Josh is the only one who might know, and he's the Sphinx as far as other people's business goes." He looked around. They weren't within listening distance of any of the others, who were huffing behind them. "Interested?" he asked.

"Not the way you mean," he said even as he knew it wasn't exactly truthful. But then Jubal would know that. The very fact he'd asked about her was a giveaway. "I shouldn't be," he corrected. "But she lights up wherever she goes."

"She does that," Jubal said. "Be cautious, my friend. Covenant Falls can be dangerous to bachelorhood."

"You seem to be content with it," Ross said.

"I am. I have a life with Lisa and the kids I never thought was possible for me. I was pretty much a broken-down wreck when I arrived here. Those years as a prisoner broke me physically and mentally. Then I met Lisa and her brother and sister, and they chased away the shadows. Jacko clinched it. They certainly changed my life." He paused, then added, "That doesn't mean it works that way for everyone. I don't want to see Susan get hurt again."

It was obviously a warning. Ross nodded. "I don't, either," he said.

Then he had to ask, "What happened before?"

"I don't know all of it. Just that it was bad enough that she's avoiding any meaningful relationships now."

Another not so subtle warning.

But Jubal was right.

There was no place to go for Susan and himself.

He just nodded, and Jubal dropped to the back of the pack.

Kate and another vet took Jubal's place alongside him. "Ready to pick up the pace?" he asked her.

"Sure," Kate said. Her companion nodded, and Ross

sensed a challenge going on between them. A budding romance?

"Go for it," he said, and dropped back as the jog turned into a race. He and Jubal stayed to the back, making sure no one was left behind or having a problem.

Jubal glanced at him. "We have a good race between those two," he said.

"Yeah, I think we do. Any guess as to the winner?"

"Kate," they said in unison.

They were right.

When they arrived back at the bunkhouse, Jubal took Ross aside. "Want a private tour of the property? Has to be on horseback."

"I saw some of it with you before," Ross said, puzzled.

"There's much more," Jubal said. "It will take a little more than an hour."

Ross hesitated. The stable was still a reservoir of bad memories. Dammit, he had to get over it someday. Still, he fought it. "I'm not that sure of my riding."

"I watched you," Jubal replied. "You have a good seat. You looked comfortable enough."

"What about Hobo?"

"Danny will look after him."

Ross had no more excuses. He simply nodded. His hands started to sweat as they walked in. Shadows seemed to fall over the interior. He stiffened, fought off the inclination to turn around and leave.

He stopped suddenly as they walked under a beam. *Steady*. No creak. No shadows from a lone battery-operated lantern.

"Ross?"

Had Jubal guessed the turmoil inside?

"Sorry," he said. "Just paused to look at the black horse. He's a handsome guy."

"He is that," Jubal said. "Gentle, as well. He belongs to Luke. Damien is one of his best teaching horses."

Ross nodded. He walked to Cajun's stall and stopped while Jubal went to Jacko's stall. Cajun nuzzled him, looking for a carrot. Memories began to fade. "Sorry," Ross said. "I was distracted. I'll give you a carrot on the way out." There was still a stiffness in his voice as it suddenly occurred to him that he'd been talking to animals a lot lately.

After saddling their horses, Jubal and Ross led them outside before mounting. Riley stood near a tree and looked as if he was waiting for someone. He approached Ross.

"I came to see my horse," Riley said but he just stood there as Jubal mounted Jacko and moved out of hearing distance.

"Riley," Ross said. "Can I help you with anything?"

"Can I talk to you later?" Riley asked.

"Sure," Ross said. He glanced at his watch. "I'll be back no later than 9:00 a.m. What's good for you?"

"Nine is good," Riley replied. "Thanks."

"Where do you want to meet?"

"Outside the bunkhouse?"

Ross didn't have any appointments until after lunch. He'd planned on mostly watching this morning. "Sounds good to me."

Riley nodded.

Jubal led the way as the two of them followed the path taken on Ross's first ride, then continued along the stream to a smaller paddock where several mares grazed with their youngsters. Straight ahead was a small lake at the foot of the mountain.

A neat log cabin surrounded by tall aspens sat on the far side of the lake. "There's ten acres here," Jubal said. "The former owners of my ranch built it as a guesthouse for their grown children and their families." He led the way to the cabin and the two of them dismounted. They tied the horses to one of the trees and Ross followed Jubal to the cabin.

The door opened to a large living area. The interior was rustic with log walls, a rock fireplace on one side and a picture window facing the lake. It was furnished with a long sofa and several lounge chairs. To the right was a kitchen with a stove, fridge, lots of cupboards and room for a large table. A hallway led to two nice-sized bedrooms and a bathroom.

"And you are showing this to me because…?" Ross didn't really have to ask. He knew.

"Because it might make a good base for you."

Ross stared at Jubal. "You barely know me."

"I'm a quick judge of character," Jubal replied. "And Josh really likes you. You fit in well here. It was obvious yesterday."

"I don't care about having a base," Ross said as he looked around. If he did, though, it was perfect for one person. Or two.

Where in the hell did that thought come from?

"You don't need to answer," Jubal said, ignoring Ross's statement. "Just let it simmer. We have a terrific vet community here. You could continue to travel to jobs as much as you want but you would have a home base. Help us out whenever you're here."

Ross hesitated. There was a certain logic to it. Jubal

had probably wanted to meet him before offering the cabin—rather than the inn—for his stay in Covenant Falls. He looked around. Horses grazed beyond the lake and now the morning sun spread a streak of gold across the water. Peaceful. Although it was only a few minutes by horse from Jubal's stables, it could have been miles away.

"Is it for sale?" Damn if he knew why he was asking the question.

"Could be. Could be leased. Could just be here whenever you worked with our program. You can even raise a few horses of your own," Jubal tempted. He hesitated, then added, "We just want you to know it's here and available."

"We?"

"Josh and me. He wanted you and me to meet before he suggested it. I'm all for it. It's wasted now, and I don't want it to go outside this group." With that, they headed back to the stables.

This group. It was a generous offer. Ross mulled it over as they rode back. It kinda made sense if he wasn't deadset against permanence. He liked everyone he'd met and admired what they were doing. He didn't think the offer was spontaneous. He suspected Josh had engineered the whole thing—Jubal and the others just wanted to meet him first. And they did that Sunday night.

There was still that sense of dread as he and Jubal approached the stable. But maybe now it wouldn't be as debilitating as earlier. He had gotten through it yesterday and survived without making a fool of himself. Maybe the ranch had been healing for him.

They dismounted outside the stable, and he led Cajun inside. The horse nuzzled his neck as they entered, and

Ross wondered if he sensed his rider's unease that still plagued him. Ross made himself concentrate. *Unsaddle the horse. Cool him down. Don't forget a carrot.*

"Thanks," he told Cajun as he gave him the carrot. When he'd replaced the riding equipment in the tack room, he sought out Riley.

The bunkhouse was empty except for the vet. He was bouncing a ball on the Ping-Pong table. "Hey there," Ross said. "You any good at that?"

"Used to be. Probably the only thing I was ever good at. When I was in the service, I was the champion for my unit. Do you know that it's now an Olympic sport, or so I heard."

"Nope. I didn't know that."

Riley put the paddle down. "Can we go outside?"

"Sure. I know just the place," Ross said. "We can walk."

Ross set the pace. They walked across one empty pasture until they reached a second, where four mares looked after foals frolicking at their heels.

Riley smiled for the first time.

"It makes me relax, too," Ross said. He sat on the fence and Riley did the same. "I saw them yesterday," Ross said. "There's something peaceful about watching them. There's such unbounded enthusiasm for life."

Riley nodded, staring at a foal and its mother. "I have a kid," he said. "My ex-wife doesn't want me around him. She's talking about getting a restraining order. I think I should go home."

"Why doesn't she want you around him?"

His head ducked. "I scared the hell out of them. I thought I was back in Afghanistan and was waving my gun. It wasn't loaded. I made sure of that, but it frightened Doug, my kid. He's eight." He kept his head down. "It wasn't the first time."

Ross suspected there was more to it than that.

"Had she mentioned a a restraining order before?"

He nodded.

"She knows you're here?"

He nodded again.

"What will she do if you go home early?"

"Probably make it worse," he admitted.

Ross nodded. "Good thinking." He paused, and then added, "I'm not an attorney or psychologist," he said. "I'm not married and never have been so I have no background or qualification to give you advice. But as a friend, and I hope that we are friends, I think you need to prove to her you're trying. That means staying here. Work like hell with your horse, work with me on developing a physical therapy regimen that establishes self-discipline. Talk to the others here. Know you are not alone. We all have some of the same problems."

Riley nodded. "I rarely talk about mine."

"That's one of our problems," Ross said. "Few of us do. We don't want to look weak. But PTSD is not a weakness, not unless you think a good percentage of the military is weak. Along with a sizable number of civilians who have experienced trauma, physical or mental."

Riley stared at him. "What…what are your…problems? If you don't mind telling me?"

"Barns," Ross said simply. "And you're one of the very few people who know that. I don't even have the excuse of it being caused by battle." He had to be honest if he expected the vets to trust him.

"Barns?" Riley looked disbelieving.

"Something that happened there when I was a kid. I get flashbacks going into a barn or stable."

"But you did it today. I saw you," Riley said.

"I forced myself to enter after years of avoiding them. I almost didn't come to Covenant Falls for that reason. I knew it would involve going into a barn or stable. I knew I would relive events I've tried to forget. But I owed a friend."

"I keep seeing my buddy bleeding out and I couldn't stop it," Riley said. "I should have done more, something, anything," Riley blurted out. "I can't get him out of my mind."

"Did you tell your wife about it?"

"No. I couldn't. It was my fault. I trusted the attacker. I should have known there was something wrong with…" He stopped. "I can't forget my buddy's face and wonder, why him? Why not me?"

"I know," Ross replied. "I was a medic and I remember the face of every soldier I lost. I have questions I ask myself. Could I have done more for them? If I had known more, could I have saved them? So you're not alone. That's why Jubal started this program, to let you know you're not—we're not—alone."

Riley nodded.

"Anytime you want to talk, I'm here," Ross finished. "I hope you stay."

He stood and together they walked back to the bunkhouse. Upon returning, he pulled out his cell phone and saw that there were several messages. One was from Josh. He called back.

It was answered immediately. "Ross," his friend said, "we haven't had any time to get together. Can you come over for steaks tonight?"

"Sure, sounds good." He'd heard from Jubal and others about Josh's steaks. He also couldn't quite believe the former grouchy staff sergeant was married with a stepson and a bunch of dogs. "Can I bring Hobo?" he asked.

"Of course. Nick would be most unhappy if you didn't. He really took to Hobo, but then he really takes to everything with a tail, even lizards, much to Eve's dismay."

"What time?"

"Seven. Travis will be here with his wife, Jenny. You'll really like her. She's a former war correspondent and now a syndicated writer of travel adventures. She can probably tell you the best places to visit on your Pacific Coast trip."

For some reason, he hadn't thought about that trip in the past several days. He'd been too busy looking after his guys and Hobo.

"I'll be there. Just give me the directions."

There was a brief silence. "It's complicated," he said. "Susan's coming from the inn. No sense in you both driving."

No sense? He sensed a conspiracy but he didn't want to say anything. "Sounds good," he said. "Thanks."

"I'll see you at seven," Josh said.

Ross ended the call. He had thought about riding this afternoon but he wasn't eager to go into the stable again despite his talk with Riley earlier—not after last night's flashback. And he was tired after a sleepless night. A relaxed dinner with an old friend was exactly what he needed. He also wanted to thank Travis. He'd been impressed with his notes about other programs.

And, dammit, he looked forward to seeing Susan again. He missed her and found himself looking for her.

Ross admitted to himself she was partly why he wasn't

as enthused about the trip up the coast as he was four days ago. He was already invested in the ranch's guests. They had almost given up on being happy again. And he liked the comradery he felt with them, with Josh and Jubal. He hadn't realized how much he'd missed being with army buddies.

He took Hobo for a walk, such as it was. The little guy was bouncing back quickly. He'd mastered walking with the new splint and was exhibiting curiosity. He wanted to sniff everything, as if he hadn't had much opportunity in his past life. But then he would look back suddenly, and Ross knew the dog was checking on him, making sure he was still there.

He was getting used to Hobo. Even thinking, maybe, about finding a way to keep him.

Then he remembered how everything and everyone he loved had dissolved into thin air. He'd sworn to himself that he would never depend on anyone again, never risk his heart. It was why he was always on the move. Being a traveling PT kept life interesting. He made good money. Saw new places. Every job was a challenge, an adventure. He liked meeting people as long as everything stayed on a temporary basis.

Susan was not a temporary person. She was a salt of the earth type of person. She was a giver. It was a mystery why she wasn't married now with two or three or four kids.

He sighed. Apparently keeping away from her wasn't an option during the next ten days, including at dinner tonight. The image of her laughing with one of the vets yesterday wouldn't leave his mind. What would it be like to have that kind of sunshine in his life?

But then he would risk losing it.

* * *

Susan worked on the payroll. It was her least favorite thing to do. It was reality, trying to balance income with expenses and provide what she thought should be a decent wage.

She badly wanted to give Mark, Judy and Janet raises. In lieu of that, she tried to compensate with flexible hours, overtime pay, free meals and whatever else she could do for them.

She'd given Janet the morning off. She could handle the desk and telephone as well as paying bills and doing the payroll. Her mind, though, was in a different place. It was about two miles down the road.

It had taken all her willpower not to join the morning run at sunrise, then ride with some of the vets. But there was no question that she'd neglected the inn and she needed time away from Ross Taylor. He'd become far too important to her in a very short time.

The phone rang. Caller ID reported it was Josh.

"Hi," he said. "Surprised to find you there."

"You're a tough taskmaster, boss," she replied.

"Ha!" Josh said. "Jubal said you've been invaluable these past few days at the ranch."

"You know how I love horses and your vets."

"I do. And yet you're working this morning at the inn."

"*Your* inn," she reminded him.

"There is that. But I think it's time you had some fun and relaxation."

"And what would that be?"

"Grilled steaks at my house."

She loved his steaks. She didn't know what he did to them. It was a state secret, he contended, but there were none better. "Anyone else?" she asked suspiciously.

"Travis and Jenny."

"And..."

"Ross," Josh replied.

"You are not fixing me up, are you, Josh? You know how I feel about that. I can manage my own life, thank you."

"No. Swear it. It's just he doesn't know anyone here."

"He knows a lot of people now," Susan countered. "He's the Pied Piper at the ranch. He's got all the vets and most of the staff out running at 6:00 a.m."

"I heard about that," he said with amusement. "But he hasn't seen Travis in a long time, I suspect. And you and Jenny are friends. That's it."

"You swear?"

"Yes."

"Do I get a bonus for coming?"

"On top of the steaks?"

"Yes."

He sighed over the phone. "What about that painting you want for the inn library."

"Done," she said quickly. She'd been begging for a certain Western painting for months. It would complement the many Western novels and historical literature available there.

"You are very devious, Ms. Hall. Can you give Ross a ride over here? That bike might not startle Jubal's horses, but I don't think Beauty and the Beast will be as understanding."

"Nothing bothers those horses much," she shot back, "and what if Ross plans to stay late at the ranch today?"

"Jubal will take care of that."

"I smell a scheme here," she said, "but you're the boss. I'll pick him up at the inn at ten to seven. *If* he's here."

"Thanks," Josh said. "I've been wanting Ross and Travis to meet up sooner, but Travis is in the middle of football season. He wants to catch up with Ross."

"You're going to have an entire army company here by the time you get through."

"Makes you feel safe, doesn't it?" Josh said.

"I felt safe before. Not so much since you called."

"See you in a few hours, Susan."

"Yes, sir."

Susan hung up. She wondered if Ross was going to co-operate. Probably. Josh usually got his way. She smiled. The former Ranger staff sergeant was determined to grow Covenant Falls and make it a haven for veterans. He certainly wasn't above a little bribery, like a painting for the inn library.

But it certainly put a crimp in her plan to avoid Ross Taylor.

Chapter 12

Susan discarded several blouses and shirts before choosing her least favorite. It did nothing for her.

Good.

She liked Ross Taylor far more than she should.

Hadn't she learned her lesson about quick infatuation? She'd been twenty-one when she met Richard, one of the management staff of the hotel where she'd been hired as a junior executive, a very junior executive. It was her first job after receiving her degree in hotel management... She'd promised herself after a nightmare marriage that she would never be vulnerable again and now she was falling heads over heels for a wanderer.

She knew Josh's intent tonight. He'd never been subtle. Once he married, he thought everyone else should also enjoy marital bliss. Especially if it was someone he wanted to keep in Covenant Falls. The supper tonight was undoubtedly part of a plan to keep Ross here. She wasn't particularly happy about being the bait to do it.

But she also always enjoyed an evening at his house. She'd been friends with his wife, Eve, since they were in preschool together. She was crazy about Nick, and Josh's dog, Amos, as well as the motley group of misfit pets Nick had collected, including Dizzy, a crazy cat who loved spinning around in circles. And last but not least, she loved Josh's steaks. She wondered, though, if Ross was aware of his friend's manipulative impulses.

The other lure was Hobo. She'd enjoyed being around the little dog and watching Ross's conflict over him. He wasn't winning that battle, and she liked him the more for it. Like Josh and Jubal, Ross was a protector, whether they all realized it or not. It was in his instant rapport with the participants in the program, in his wide smile when they'd all made it back from the first run and when he joined Dennis in doing push-ups.

She was a sucker for protectors.

Darn. She exchanged her least favorite shirt for her most favorite, a royal blue that went with her eyes. But she also chose an old pair of jeans. A compromise between her cautious side and her old adventuresome spirit.

She smiled at herself in the mirror. Maybe it was time.

Josh's obvious matchmaking wasn't going to work, Ross thought as he got ready for the evening Josh had arranged.

If there were ever two people who should never be together, it was Susan and him. There were just too many damned cupids in the town. Nonetheless, he wished he had some fine-smelling aftershave.

He selected the blue denim shirt he'd bought at the

General Store and his one remaining pair of clean jeans. They were the really worn ones. Then he glanced at the khakis he'd purchased at the General Store. He hadn't known why he'd bothered.

He shook his head. This was the dumbest internal argument he'd ever had with himself. *Admit it. You want to look half-civilized.* He resisted temptation. Instead of changing clothes, he combed his unruly hair into submission.

Once ready, he took Hobo for a walk. Hobo immediately did his business and looked up to him for approval. The dog had already recognized him as an easy mark. Josh had obviously taken note of it.

He looked at his watch. It was almost time to meet Susan. He was glad Hobo had been included in the invitation. A shield. Unless of course, Hobo was part of a conspiracy, which at the moment seemed altogether plausible.

Susan was at the desk talking to Mark. She looked up and her smile blew straight through the shadows of doubt.

She wore all blue. Nothing dressy but a well-cut royal blue shirt and jeans. Her hair was in a long braid as usual but when she smiled, there was a twinkle in her eyes as if they shared a secret. Hobo made his little throaty noises in greeting. *Traitor.*

"Hi," he said.

"Do you feel trapped?" she said in the forthright tone that always intrigued him.

"No," he heard himself say. And oddly enough, he no longer did. There would certainly be enough distractions at Josh's house to keep them apart. "You look great."

"Thank you. You're not bad yourself," she said with

a grin. "Which will suit Josh. You know he's trying to match-make."

"I sorta got that idea."

"Should we go along or put him straight?" she asked.

He wondered what "put him straight" meant exactly. Was there anything to put straight? They'd just met and yet he couldn't deny the electricity that sparked between them when he least expected it. He couldn't deny he wanted to spend more time with her, or that he wanted to kiss her again in the worst way.

"I'll try to let him down easily," he said.

"Good luck."

When they arrived at Josh's house, Nick immediately cornered Ross and Hobo as the boy's tribe of dogs introduced themselves in different ways. One a lick, one a bark, one a nudge. One tried to jump into Ross's lap until Hobo growled and the offender slunk off.

Hobo was getting his mojo back.

Despite Susan's warning, she was whisked off to the kitchen by Eve, leaving Ross in Josh's clutches.

"Ever think about settling down?" Josh asked.

"Nope," Ross said easily. "Never have."

"Neither had I until I came here," he said. "Shocked the hell out of me."

"I have to admit I never thought you, of all people, would settle down," Ross agreed.

"There was one battle too many," Josh said. "When David died and I was wounded, all I wanted to do was crawl up in a hole. It was finding his dog that kept me from doing it. Then I met Eve. She wouldn't let me do it, either."

Ross nodded but didn't say anything.

"Don't worry. I'm not going to try to convince you to

stay, although you would have a place here if you did. The guys really like you. Luke, Jubal and me are the instructors, but from the day you stepped on Jubal's ranch, you were one of 'them.' The vets. I don't know how you do it, but you make hard work fun. We would like to keep you here."

"Jubal already showed me the cabin," Ross said. "There's not enough work here to keep me in beer," Ross pointed out as Josh handed him one. "Besides, I chose being a traveling PT because I *wanted* to travel. I like the variety. And it pays well."

"I'm not going to press you. Just wanted you to know you have options."

The rest of the night went quickly. Travis arrived in a football uniform shirt and Jenny was, as described, a great storyteller.

So was Eve. She kept the conversation going, mentioning that the origins of the Camel Trail Inn started here at the dinner table. "It's been Susan's baby since." Then she changed the subject to Covenant Falls and its story.

It was at dessert when Eve asked, "Have you been to the falls yet?"

"No. I've been pretty busy at the ranch."

"I heard about that. You even have Jubal running again. Josh should join you."

"Great idea," Ross said. "You're getting a little…"

Josh's glower stopped him. "Don't say it," Josh warned.

Ross grinned. "I think I've worn out my welcome fast." He looked at his watch. "We should leave soon. I have observations to record while they're still in my head. And I imagine Susan needs to feed the terror that is her cat."

"You really should see them," Josh persisted.

"I read the brochure. I understand you'll be taking the guys there on horseback for the wilderness trip."

"Yeah. When Jubal and Luke think they're ready."

"That's quite a group that's come together," Ross said. "Rangers, Special Services and a SEAL."

"It makes for good poker games," Josh said. "Every Monday night at the community center except during the weeks our participants are here." He changed the subject. "You really do need to see the falls before you leave."

"I'll make a point of it," he said.

"And now, I'd better get him home," Susan said, "and me. These late nights are not helping my relationship with Vagabond."

"That is the world's ugliest cat," Travis said with a grin.

"It's all in the eyes of the beholder," Susan protested. "I think she looks as if she has character."

"A bad one," Josh tossed in.

"You two just don't appreciate individuality," Susan replied with mock outrage. "And since you all see fit to slander my cat, we *are* leaving."

It was Ross's signal to stand. They all said goodbye and he followed her out to her Jeep.

"Tired?" Susan asked as she started the car.

"Not really," he said. He felt, instead, invigorated.

"Want to drive up to the falls tonight?"

"Can we see anything?"

"The moon's almost full and I have a lantern in the car. There could be some teenagers."

"We could pretend like we got lost," he said.

She laughed, and he loved the sound of it. Like bells.

Damn, it was all he needed tonight. Falls and bells and a woman who made him laugh.

But it was a fine night with a fresh breeze and a sky

of a million stars. He didn't want to go back to his room, as pleasant as it was, alone. Which was out of character. He usually didn't mind being alone.

They passed a place called the Rusty Nail Saloon. "That's Josh's favorite place, and they deliver to the inn if you get hungry. They have great hamburgers and fries. Very veteran friendly."

About fifteen minutes later, she turned at a big sign announcing The Falls of Covenant Falls. "We're a fair distance from the town itself," Ross noted.

"We're still in the city limits. It's a long story but, to make it short, the founder of the town had a lot of political clout and was able to extend the city limits to include the falls. Go online and search Covenant Falls. Most of the history is there."

He was intrigued, especially after Eve's storytelling earlier. The road twisted around until they reached a parking area. She took a lantern from the back, but the moon was bright enough to see a trail without it.

Hobo was sound asleep, and Ross decided to leave the dog in the car. As they walked a path that looked as if it was going into a forest, he heard the roaring of the falls. She led him to a railing and he looked down. A river ran swiftly below. His hand caught hers and curled around her fingers. She looked up at him, the very blue eyes searching his face.

"You look great in moonlight," he said.

"So do you, craggy face and all."

"Craggy?" He raised an eyebrow in question.

"In a good, sexy way."

"I don't know whether to be insulted or not."

"Not," she said. "I like craggy."

Their eyes were locked on each other, their fingers

tightening around the other's. Knowing it was reckless and stupid, he used his free hand to touch her face and trace the curves. He lifted her chin until their eyes met. "You're so darn…irresistible," he said. "I've been trying to stay away and, dammit, it's not working very well."

Especially tonight when I actually agreed to visit a waterfall at night. How reckless could he get? But the words accepting her invite had just popped out. He wanted to be alone with her and not at the inn where someone might take notice. Word traveled too quickly in Covenant Falls.

He'd lied to himself about keeping a distance from her. He hadn't tried that hard. He ignored his instincts because he truly liked her, was attracted to her, but that was before he realized his feelings ran deeper than they should. Something inside lit like a Christmas tree whenever she came into sight.

She wasn't the kind of woman he could kiss, sleep with and leave without damaging both of them. She was the kind he'd avoided through basic training, his years in the army and the eight years since. She was the forever kind.

She looked up into his face, his eyes. He didn't know what she wanted or how she felt. Maybe she didn't feel the same warmth when he was around as he did when she was near.

Even if she did, she knew how he felt about permanence. He'd made it clear from the time they first met. She, on the other hand, was apparently sustained by permanence.

She moved away but caught his hand. "You haven't seen the waterfall yet."

"I can hear it," he replied.

She tugged his hand and they went around a heavily wooded bend, then he stopped. Water roared over a high, rocky cliff. It threw off water drops that caught the glow from the moon and glistened in the air.

He'd rarely seen anything as magical. It wasn't a word he'd used before but nothing else fit.

"Why isn't anyone else here?"

"It's a school night and most parents wouldn't want their kids driving up that road at night." She paused, then added, "In the daytime, a rainbow hovers over it. The park is usually packed on weekends."

"And Covenant Falls has it all to itself?"

"Until recently. We're trying to change that."

"Why?"

"We need more residents and visitors. We have too many young people leaving because there's not many opportunities here. It's why I left."

"And yet you returned."

"Yes," she said, "I did. But I should never have left. Maybe that's why I want the town to grow. It's a great place to live. I don't want other young people to leave because they can't find jobs."

He thought about another small town, one that wasn't able to adjust. It was just an empty place in the road now. Fear had torn it apart, had torn his family apart.

"What are you thinking?" she asked as if she was reading his mind. "You look very serious," she observed.

"About another town, years ago," he said. "It didn't fare as well."

She was silent for a moment, then moved closer and leaned against him. He noted how well she fit there.

"Your home?" she asked softly.

He nodded. "For a while."

"And then?"

He usually passed off questions about his childhood by shrugging, but now he wanted her to know things he'd never told anyone else. "A lot of places. Seven of them before I graduated from high school and enlisted."

"Were you in a Military family?" she asked.

"No," he said without elaborating. He'd always been ashamed that no one had wanted him, and that he'd been tossed between relatives like an unwanted pair of shoes.

"Is that why you're uncomfortable with staying anywhere long? No roots."

"Part of it, I suppose," he admitted. "But I also like traveling and meeting all kinds of people."

"You really do like it?" she asked.

"I do," he said with certainty, crushing the seed of doubt growing in his mind.

As if reading his mind, she lifted herself on tiptoe and put her arms around him. "I like *you*," she said, then ruined it by adding, "You're really helping with the guys."

"Is that the only reason?"

"Are you fishing for compliments, Mr. Taylor?"

"Yeah," he admitted.

"Okay, you look like a bear, but you're really a softie."

"My patients wouldn't agree. I can be fierce."

"Only because you care," Susan said. "I like other things, as well. I like the manly walk."

"Manly walk?"

"Like James Arness in *Gunsmoke*."

He gave her a disbelieving look. "You watch *Gunsmoke*?"

"Watch the reruns. I love them. And not just to learn how to mount a horse."

"And I look like I'm going to a gunfight?"

"Well you look like no one should start one with you. You ride better than you should after a few days. You have all the earmarks of a real honest-to-God cowboy."

"And you have moonlight in your hair," he said, focusing the conversation on her. He didn't want to talk about himself. He wanted to talk about Susan. He leaned over and pulled the long braid over her shoulder. He wondered how it looked loose and spread over a pillow.

Stop thinking about it.

But he couldn't stop himself from leaning over, lifting her chin and tracing his fingers over her face, photographing it in his mind.

She reached up to his face in turn, studying it. It was as if she was looking into his soul, searching for something she believed was there, and his heart sped faster. He'd had relationships. Short ones based on the knowledge that it would be over in a few days or, at the longest, a few weeks. He'd made them light and fun, and the second a relationship seemed to turn serious for either partner, he left.

But now he leaned down and touched his lips to hers, and it wasn't fun and games. He felt, instead, as if the world turned upside down.

His arms went around her and the kiss deepened. There was something about the moonlight on the falls—about a midnight-blue sky with a thousand stars and the music of the water tumbling over the cliff. It was an unreal world.

He felt caught in a whirlwind he couldn't control. There were only those blue eyes and a vulnerability mixed with uncertainty and desire. She should be untouchable for him. Still, he couldn't make himself step back. She felt good, too damn good, and he realized how he'd been damned lonely for that kind of warmth. He reveled in the kiss, her response to it. Her body melded into his, and her lips opened to his. Passion blazed between them.

She slipped her hands around his neck and drew him closer. His body responded accordingly. He was befuddled by its longing, his longing, and was locked someplace between disbelief and enchantment. With a groan, he released her lips and studied her face.

Her blue eyes glistened with wonder. Her body trembled against his, telegraphing a need as strong as his own.

Move away. His brain commanded but his body didn't obey. She aroused every masculine instinct in him, and he wanted desperately to take her back to the inn and make love.

Damn, it had been there since the beginning. The whiff of attraction, the passing touch, the meeting of eyes, the smiles that turned to laughter.

He felt caught in a whirlwind he couldn't control.

How could his world be turned upside down so quickly?

Physical attraction was great, but how long did it last? He couldn't deny, though, that something powerful was drawing him to her and had since he first met her.

Her hand reached up and touched his face in a wondering kind of way as if she too was amazed at the combustibility between the two of them.

His breath caught and he did what he'd wanted to do since the first time she'd teased him about Hobo in the bathroom. His lips touched hers lightly at first, then with fierceness he couldn't control.

She leaned into the embrace and responded with a fervor of her own.

He forced himself to stop before he did something

both of them might regret. He stepped back and regarded her somberly. "You're thinking too hard," she said, once again reading his thoughts.

"I do that sometimes," he said. "It's one of my failings."

"You give the appearance of the opposite. Carefree. Life is an adventure."

"I have a few responsible moments," he said wryly and his fingers tightened around hers as he said the words. "And you. Have you had carefree moments?"

"Oh yes. Once. I grew up here and on the whole it was a great life. Horseback riding, Skiing. Everyone knew everyone and it was safe. I didn't really have a father. He left my mother when I was a kid but I was surrounded in love by my mother and her family.

"But when it came to college, I wanted what you have. Freedom. Adventures. I thought a degree in hospitality management would give it to me. I envisioned working in hotels here and abroad. I wanted to explore the big world. After college, I accepted a job at a casino resort in Vegas. A trainee position that could lead to a permanent marketing job."

Her hand tightened on his. "It was like wonderland. Great food. Celebrities. A good salary and the promise of a better one. A great guy who was a manager in marketing."

Ross noted a change in her voice when she said the last *great* and pulled her closer to him.

"I fell in love, or thought I did," she said. "Richard was my boss. He was helpful, attentive, good-looking, great with guests. If I detected anything wrong it was his overprotectiveness. But at the time I was in a dazzling world, having dinner with the top talent who played at the casino and other celebrities. He pressed marriage way too soon, but I had stars in my eyes." She halted.

His hand tightened on hers. He sensed what was coming.

"I was good at my trainee job. I had a lot of marketing ideas that I passed on to Richard. "I was pretty naive and should have suspected something when he told everyone I was his 'country girl.' But I thought I was in love, and stupidly married him. It was the biggest mistake in my life."

She took a deep breath. "He convinced me to keep it secret, that the management did not allow married couples in the same department. Eight months after our marriage, I was fired.

"I was stunned. I didn't understand why until I talked to a friend who was a secretary in the marketing department. She told me that our marriage had been reported, and Richard admitted it. He also took credit for all my work. I was fired but he was not. He thought, though, that I could still produce marketing ideas and plans for which he could take sole credit.

"I finally figured out that was why he married me. His job was in trouble. He was a glad-hander, but not very imaginative. Marrying me was a way to keep innovative projects coming.

When I finally put everything together, I left him, filed for divorce and looked for other jobs. But he was vindictive and tried to sabotage every prospective job. He was pretty successful at it."

Ross's arms tightened around her. "One tough girl from the country," he interjected.

"No one else thought so. Wonderland turned into hell," she said.

"I divorced him and took back my maiden name. He retained his job and found a new bright assistant that created work he put forth as his own. I tried to get other jobs in the area but he always heard about it and managed to ruin my reputation. He even found me three states away in small boutique hotel. And thus my thirst for adventure ended."

"I would like to meet him someday," Ross said. He hoped his tone conveyed it would not be a pleasant meeting.

"He's not worth a second thought," she said. "I heard from a friend he'd been fired. I know managers are credited with work done by their subordinates, but he always claimed they were his alone, that he was the creative person behind them."

"Where is he now?" Ross asked.

"At the ends of the earth, I hope. He was eventually fired. What bothers me is how I could have been so... stupid."

"One thing you are not is stupid," Ross interjected. "You're the most capable and caring woman I've met."

She smiled at that. "I think you're prejudiced because I let you give your dog a bath in my house."

"Well, there is that," he said with a grin. "For some dumb reason, I was quite besotted with that mischievous smile when you left me there and escaped." Then the smile disappeared as he returned to the previous topic. "Did you ever see him again?"

She shook her head. "No. I came limping back to Covenant Falls. Eve, who was city manager at the time and childhood friend, hired me to do some promotion for the city and help get state grants for the town. Covenant Falls gave me my life back, along with restoring my self-confidence. I won't ever hide or run away again. He's part of the reason I learned karate. So watch it, mister."

"Did he ever hit you?" he asked, ready to go find the bastard wherever he may be.

"Our last encounter, he did. I hit him back. It was very satisfying."

Her dark blue eyes smoldered. Color rushed into her cheeks and she looked beautiful in that moment. Like a warrior.

The electricity that had been sizzling between them ignited. Her eyes were anything but cool now.

All the air in his lungs expelled in a gasp. He felt her edging toward him, and his arms went around her.

His lips touched hers and explosions rocked him to the toes.

He was stunned. He'd vowed not to get involved and now he was doing exactly that. He was stunned even more when her body melded into his, and her lips opened to him and passion blazed between them…

All of Susan's good intentions evaporated as he kissed her.

The attraction between them had built steadily since that first night. She'd tried to ignore it, but it was there, growing stronger each hour she spent with him. She'd gravitated toward him even as she vowed to stay away.

The second his lips touched hers she knew she wanted this to happen.

She looked at him helplessly. She was only too aware of her words spoken only minutes before.

His lips left hers, his gaze searching her face, his fingers touching her cheek. Then he leaned down again and his lips brushed hers. This time it was a tentative touch.

Tender, yet crackling. Every nerve in her seemed to come alive. The core of her warmed.

"I know," he said in a hoarse voice. "Bad idea. Terrible idea. But, dammit, I wanted to kiss you." His thumb went to her cheeks, stroking them lightly. Then he bent down and his lips touched her forehead before moving— very, very slowly to her mouth. Explosions rocked her to her toes.

There was restraint in his kiss. His tongue moved slowly, seeking a response and finding it. One that was as needy as his. He pulled her against him and her body hugged his, setting every part of her ablaze.

"This is not wise," he said again.

"No," she agreed but stretched up on tiptoe and circled his neck with her arms. "But I don't care."

The air was thick with emotion. His fingers curled around her neck, and her body seemed to melt into his. He kissed her again, this time more gently. Lips touched lips with featherlike gentleness, each of them prolonging the discovery as the kiss deepened, each step relished as they explored each other.

His hands loosened the elastic on the long braid and his fingers combed through it until it tumbled free.

He bent down to renew the kiss when the sound of approaching cars startled both of them. They looked at each other, then broke apart and tried to look proper. Like friends.

She suspected they wouldn't fool anyone, that they looked guilty as hell, which was stupid. They were adults but, darn it, she felt like a teenager caught doing something she shouldn't.

"Curses," Ross said. "I don't suppose we can sneak away."

"'Curses?'" she asked with a sudden humor that made her smile. "A bit old-fashioned, are we?"

Did he always have to surprise her?

"And to answer your question," she added, "no, we can't sneak away and get to my Jeep unless we hide in the woods."

"Your face is flushed," he said.

"Your hair is mussed," she replied. "I think we're getting caught red-handed."

Three teenage couples were laughing as they turned into the picnic area. They stopped suddenly when they saw Susan and Ross. Apparently they'd assumed her Jeep belonged to someone in their age group.

They appeared to be juniors or seniors. They stared at Ross and Susan with amazement, then dismay.

"It's okay," Susan said to them. She recognized them as local high school students. "We're leaving and since it doesn't look like you have alcohol, I'm not saying anything if you don't. Kids, this is Ross Taylor. He's helping out at New Beginnings. I'm showing him the falls."

The kids snickered.

Ross held his hand out to Susan and she took it. With as much dignity as they could muster, they took the path and walked around the stand of trees before looking at each other, nearly choking with laughter.

"I think we had guilty faces," he said with a grin. "We'll probably be the topic of conversation tomorrow."

"You know small towns too well," she quipped back. "But I don't think so. The horror on their faces meant they probably weren't supposed to be here."

"I think we'll find out which of us is right very quickly," he said. "Want to make a bet?"

"Done," she said.

Chapter 13

Hobo gave them a frantic tail-wagging welcome when they reached Susan's Jeep, but despite the lightness of their departure from the falls, they were silent for much of the drive back to the inn.

Susan wasn't sure what had happened in those minutes in the moonlight except that the ground seemed to shift under her. Her solid foundation was failing her.

Previously, her mother and Josh were the only two people who knew what happened in Vegas, but now it was important he knew she could take care of herself. She'd been shocked when Josh asked her to manage the hotel after she'd made some suggestions during construction and she felt she had to tell him.

The inn had become her life. From the moment Josh mentioned it, she knew to her bones what she wanted to do with it. And she had. After the first year, Josh had given her a free hand.

She'd relished every moment. She practically lived in the inn, much to Vagabond's displeasure. She'd ordered the furnishings, the linens, the napkins with the legend of the Covenant Falls camels, created the dinner menus with a cook she chose. She created the website and artwork for the signage.

It was her future. After returning to Covenant Falls, she knew she wasn't leaving again. The Camel Trail Inn was her salvation.

"Now you know my life story, what about yours?" she asked after several pregnant moments in the car. "Fair is fair. You said you moved a lot?"

"There's not much to tell," he said. "I was passed between relatives who really didn't want another kid in the house. I didn't help much. I was pretty angry."

"And now you're one of the most laid-back people I've met," she said.

"Ah, the army did that. It didn't tolerate bad behavior. After a brief rebellion, I was tested, and the powers that be sent me through army medic training. I had a natural bent for it, and I could do something beneficial for my fellow soldiers rather than kill the enemy. I found something I was good at, and I found a family in the army. I discovered a lot of guys who also drew a short straw growing up. How they dealt with it was the important thing."

"Then why did you leave?"

"I tried to be the best medic I could be. But after three tours I knew I didn't want to spend twenty years trying to save people too injured for me to really help. I looked at options and liked the idea of helping people surmount injuries. That's about it."

"Except for the wandering," she corrected.

He shrugged. I like the freedom involved. I like the

travel. I like choosing the type of cases I take. They range from temporary stints at VA facilities to stuntmen and everything in between."

"How did you come to work with actors?"

A professor recommended me to an agency in Hollywood that represents PTs. My first client was an action star who needed to get back on a movie set quickly." He shrugged. "We worked well together after I nearly walked out when he didn't follow instructions.

"He passed the word, and I started getting calls from other actors and stuntmen and stuntwomen. Quick recoveries were essential. It's just a small percentage of my work although the most lucrative. It permits me to do things like Josh's New Beginnings."

They reached the inn. She wished she could have doubled the distance.

"Thanks for the guided tour," he said, as if there hadn't been a magical moment. As if, instead, nothing happened.

Something *had* happened. For her, at least. Her world had turned upside down. And she had to know if it affected him, as well.

"Have you ever thought about settling in a place like Covenant Falls?" she persisted. "I know there's not much here. Few jobs. Few conveniences. You have to drive a hundred miles to a theater or a department store. We're just now attracting a few small businesses, the largest being a specialty dog bed company with ten employees. It's mostly horse and cattle country. But it's a good place to hang your hat in between jobs."

He shrugged. "It's not a lack of conveniences that encourages me to move on. A big city doesn't attract me, either. Maybe it's because I learned it's foolish to think anything lasts."

"That's cynical," she said sadly.

"No, it's not. It's practical."

"Don't feel, and you don't get hurt? Is that it?" she asked. "Don't you miss out on a lot, then?"

He didn't answer, just put his hand on Hobo's body and lifted him out of the car and onto the ground.

She stepped out, too. She wanted to check the desk since she was here, but she didn't want him to leave for his room, either. "What are you going to do with Hobo?" she asked. "He adores you."

He turned to her. "Do you ever stop trying to save the world?"

His question was harsh as was his tone. "Not my corner of it," she shot back.

"Dammit, Susan, I can't stay! That's not what I do or who I am. And it will be unfair to Hobo. He deserves a real home."

"And you don't?" she retorted. Her heart sank. For a few magical moments, she'd felt a strong connection with him. More than a connection. Something really fine. Even grand. Something she had never felt before. She certainly hadn't felt it with Richard. That had been, admittedly, a young woman's inexperience. She hadn't felt a quarter of what she felt for Ross in a few days: the naturalness, the shared appreciation of so many things, the emotions he'd invoked during the first kiss and then their kisses tonight. They had been fireworks-worthy.

But he'd made it clear from the beginning. His freedom came first. She sensed she hadn't heard the real reason yet. A lot of moves as a kid just didn't justify it. A lot of kids experienced that.

She wasn't being fair and she knew it. He had put everyone on notice that this was a short stop, but she'd felt that maybe something changed tonight. Darn it, why had she pushed it? Maybe because she thought something was happening between them. Maybe because they'd shared a moment of intimacy. It had meant something to her. Apparently not to him.

"You could do a lot if you stayed throughout the program," she said sadly. She hated begging but something was wrong here. In the thirty minutes since they'd left the falls, he'd changed. He was cool now. "And what *about* Hobo?" she asked.

Hobo looked up at him with a doleful expression.

"Have you trained that dog?" he asked suspiciously.

"No, he's just smarter than you."

"That wouldn't be hard." His voice softened. "I should go inside. It's late. You need some sleep if you're going to make the sunrise run."

"What about you?" she asked.

"I have some work to do."

He appeared more relaxed now that the conversation had changed. There were a couple of times today he'd lowered his guard. She wanted to know more about him, a lot more, but it was as if a traffic signal suddenly turned red and was stuck on it.

"You're right," she said with a challenge in her voice. "About getting some sleep."

He nodded, picked up Hobo and walked away. He looked back at her, and she was startled to see something like pain carved in his face. But before she was sure, he turned and headed for the door of the inn.

Ross turned, watched her drive away, then walked to his room. The comforter was folded back. There was a plate of cookies next to the bed. He shared one of them with Hobo.

"What *am* I going to do with you?" he asked. In just a few days, the dog was beginning to fill out. He wouldn't fit in the little compartment on the bike much longer.

Any owner would be better than he would. He'd hurt Susan, and no one deserved that less than her. But he was beginning to care for her far too much. He'd wanted her in the worst way at the falls. If the kids hadn't shown up, he might have done something they would both regret.

He told himself he was an idiot for letting it get so far, but after her disclosure about that son of a bitch ex, he'd wanted to hold her, make love to her and tell her how stupid that guy was.

Instead, he'd rebuffed her to protect his own guarded walls. Making it worse was doing it after she'd poured out what had obviously been very painful.

Why can't I come to terms with my past when she has?

How do you tell someone that your father hanged himself and left his son to find him, that your mother then drank herself to death and left him to bounce between relatives who didn't want him and threw his father's death in his face? *He was weak. He didn't care about you.*

He'd learned how to be alone, to take care of himself, not to expect anything from anyone. It was why he was a traveling PT. He could loan out his heart on a short-term basis without fearing loss.

He filled Hobo's water dish and fed him a dish of dry dog food. The dog gobbled it up.

Ross watched Hobo eat greedily as he always did, then the dog curled up as close to him as possible. After several moments, Ross took a hot shower. For the second time in two days, he wished he had a bottle of bourbon.

When he finished, he sat in a comfortable armchair and wrote notes about his sessions with the vets. He was getting to know which ones were married, which ones were on the verge of divorce, which ones were fighting to maintain sobriety. They were coming together as a group. Helping each other. Encouraging each other. Hopefully developing long-term support relationships.

It was after midnight when he finally turned out the light. Problem was he continued to see Susan as she stood in the mist of the waterfall with that contagious smile. He still felt the magic of the embrace, the softness of her lips. She threw everything she had into whatever she did, including that kiss.

He finally rose, put on his jeans and T-shirt and headed for the door, leaving Hobo sleeping in the room. He rolled his bike out to the street so he wouldn't wake anyone. Then he mounted it. He needed to feel the wind wrap around him, the illusion of freedom it usually brought him. He rode out onto the street and then headed in the direction Susan had taken earlier.

He reached the Rusty Nail. There were several vehicles parked in front. He drove into the parking lot, parked the bike and walked into the bar. One glass of bourbon to erase the image of Susan's face when he walked away from her.

He went to the bar and selected a stool. In seconds a middle-aged guy in jeans and a pullover approached him. When he reached out a hand, Ross noticed a military tattoo on his arm.

"I'm Johnny Kay," he said. "You must be Ross Taylor," he said.

"How did you know?" Ross asked.

"News gets around fast. Heard about a big guy on a Harley helping out at New Beginnings. Not many people fit that description, at least not in Covenant Falls. I own this place and your first drink is on the house. Offer good for all current servicemen and vets. What will you have?"

"I was thinking bourbon but I'll settle for a beer since I'm on my bike. Do you have a good local one?"

"Sure do."

Ross nodded. "You're a veteran yourself," he noted. The tattoo was a giveaway.

"Iraq at the beginning," Johnny said as he took a can from a cooler and placed it in front of Ross.

The can was frosty, just as Ross liked it. He took a long swallow.

"How long you going to be here?" Johnny asked him.

"Two weeks."

"Hungry? We have good local beef."

"I had dinner at Josh's home."

Johnny just nodded. "He's a good guy and a good griller. He's really changed Covenant Falls. We're actually growing now."

"So I heard."

"How do you like the inn?"

"I haven't spent much time there," Ross replied. He would just as soon not think of the inn at the moment.

There must have been something in his tone because Johnny Kay just nodded. "Let me know if you want anything," he said and left.

There must be something to dislike about Covenant Falls but at the moment Ross couldn't think what it might be. It had a good bar, a mercantile with everything one could need, mountains, its own falls, even a rainbow apparently. Then he found its fault. It was too perfect. Who really wanted perfection?

He finished the beer, gave the owner a salute and wandered outside. For some reason his dissatisfaction with perfection grew stronger. He knew it had something to do with Susan and the way he'd messed everything up. He'd consciously hurt the last person in the world who deserved it.

He mounted the Harley and started out of the parking lot, barely missing a police car rounding a curve and turning in. His bike went down as both he and the police car swerved to avoid a crash.

He landed on the pavement, the bike on his leg.

The officer stepped out of the police car, hurried over to him and lifted the bike off his leg, then leaned down. "Ross?"

"Afraid so," Ross replied.

"Hell of a way to meet again," Covenant Falls Police Chief Clint Morgan said. " How bad is it? Can you stand?"

"I think so," Ross said, although his knee was hurting. He was pretty sure, though, that nothing was broken except his skin, which was bleeding profusely.

"Don't you want that leg checked?"

"I'm a former medic and believe me I know when something's broken or torn. My pride's taken a hit, though."

Clint disappeared to the back of the car and returned with a first aid kit. Just then Johnny appeared from the bar. "Someone said…" He stopped, saw the blood, "My God…"

"Not that bad," Ross said as he bit back a curse. "I could use a couple of towels, though." As Johnny headed back inside, Ross turned toward Clint. "How long do you think before the entire town knows?" he asked.

"Ten minutes, maybe five," Clint said. "Drove me nuts in the beginning."

Ross winced. "I had one beer."

"I can testify to that," Johnny said, who was back at his side with two wet towels.

"And some wine for dinner," Ross added honestly.

"Hell, that was hours ago," Clint said.

Damn. The police chief even knew about his dinner.

"Don't worry," Clint said. "That curve is dangerous. Too many accidents. I was just checking on Johnny before I went home. I didn't expect a Harley pulling out. I judge neither of us is responsible."

In a matter of seconds, cloth was cut away from the leg and Johnny's towels had soaked up the blood. Skin had been shaved off several spots and there was one long cut. The police chief treated it with antiseptic and bandaged it. The other occupants of the saloon wandered out and watched with interest and alcoholic sympathy. Ross groaned. No telling what the rumors would contain tomorrow.

His cell rang. It was Josh. "Are you okay?"

Damn, the grapevine was even quicker than he believed. "All but my pride," he admitted.

"Need anything?"

"Nope, but thanks."

"Does the bike need a pickup?"

"The bike's not damaged except for a few more scratches and dents."

"Okay, but I'll follow you to the inn. Jubal will have my neck if anything happens to you."

Ross hobbled to his room after arriving at the inn. He was as lame as Hobo, who was waiting at the door of his room and made small grunts of either complaint or happiness when Ross stepped inside. He half expected

Susan to appear but she didn't. He took a shower, then redressed the abrasions with items from his first aid kit.

It was after 1:00 a.m. by the time got in bed. He needed to be up at five thirty at the latest to meet the vets for the morning run.

He turned out the light but he couldn't stop rerunning the evening and night over and over again in his mind. He'd treated Susan badly. He knew nothing about healthy relationships. His military friendships were strong because his comrades lived together and fought together for years. But outside, there had been few.

He looked ahead and the future suddenly looked bleak. If he'd not swerved in time tonight, he might have died, and what would he leave behind? He wouldn't have loved or been loved. Never known what it was to father a child or, like Josh, bring one up. He had only to look at Josh and Jubal to know that each day they knew love and caring.

All he'd looked forward to was a ride up the coast. Somehow it didn't seem a very good substitute for what was being offered to him here: friends, a piece of property of his own and a woman that brightened every day just by being there.

He couldn't sleep. The realization that he may have wasted much of his life because of fear was excruciating. He'd never considered himself a coward but that's exactly what he had become.

He wondered whether he had completely destroyed the relationship with Susan in the false cause of saving her from him. It had been, instead, pure selfishness on his part.

The thought haunted him until the inn clock told him it was 5:00 a.m.

The shallow wounds were still leaking blood and he replaced bandages, then, instead of his running shorts, selected his jeans to cover them. After drinking two cups of coffee and scarfing down three rolls from the lobby, he and Hobo took off on his bike. It had dents but it was running.

The guys were already waiting in front of the bunkhouse when he arrived. They were all wearing their cowboy hats. He didn't see Susan and his heart dropped.

Riley approached him shyly, then handed him a handsome cowboy hat. It was far grander than the ones passed out on Sunday.

"We voted," Riley said, "and decided you needed one if you're leading the pack. All the guys pitched in and went to the General Store last night. They opened it just for us." He sounded very impressed about that.

Riley hesitated, glanced at the others, then added, "We thought you should know we hope you stay. That ole bike of yours isn't nearly as good as Cajun." He paused, then added shyly, "We kinda like the idea of you being here when we come back for visits."

"Yep," Danny added when Ross raised an eyebrow. "We all heard that Jubal wants you to stay, and we want you to know we hope you do. You and Hobo. Seems like you belong here." He looked a little embarrassed.

"That goes for all of us," another chipped in.

Ross was speechless. And moved. More than at any time he could remember. He knew most of these vets had little money. The hat was great but what really touched him was they meant what they said. He swallowed hard and finally managed to say, "Thank you." He placed that hat on his head. It fit perfectly. Then, in a stronger voice, he added, "Let's move."

As they started their run, he looked around for Susan. She wasn't there.

Chapter 14

Susan went directly to the inn the next morning. She knew Ross wouldn't be there. He would be at the ranch.

She'd decided not to join the run this morning and instead attend to things at the inn.

She debated fleeing Covenant Falls and driving up to Denver to peddle stories on Covenant Falls' gold mine history, but then decided that was cowardly. Darned if she was going to let Ross Taylor affect what she did or did not do.

She was still stunned from last night and his curt rejection. What had happened to the man to whom she'd poured out her heart? To whom she'd revealed the worst parts of her life?

He'd just walked away.

She'd been sleepless, trying to understand how and why he'd turned from hot to cold, from a passionate kiss to indifference, even impatience. *Do you ever stop trying to save the world?* His words kept repeating themselves, along with the curtness in his voice.

She'd spent a long time in the tub last night but she couldn't concentrate on a book or anything else. A few tears, though, wandered down her cheek.

She'd finally given up trying to read and went to bed. Vagabond seemed to understand and with a rare show of affection cuddled up next to her in bed.

At dawn she dressed, turned on the television, brewed coffee and watched the depressing morning news. When she was sure he would have left the inn, she drove over there. Sure enough, his bike was gone.

Janet looked up from the desk when she entered. "I thought you would be at Jubal's ranch."

"I decided to catch up on inn business," she said. "I've been delinquent and putting too much on you guys."

"Not at all. Mark and I are both grateful for the overtime." She leaned over the desk. "Did you hear about Mr. Taylor?"

"Hear what?"

"He was in an accident last night. Ran into Clint's police car at the Rusty Nail."

"The Rusty Nail?" she repeated, dumbfounded. "Was he hurt?"

"Just his pride, he said this morning when he came out for coffee, but he was limping a little," Janet added. "Our phone was busy this morning with everyone calling about him."

"He rode his bike?"

Janet nodded. "Can't miss that noise." She paused, then added, "I thought for sure you would be at New Beginnings, what with the ceremony and all."

"What ceremony?" Susan asked.

"You didn't know?" Janet said. "The vets all went to the General Store last evening and bought him a cowboy hat. Said he was the only one who didn't have one when they ran. Heather said they really like him. I do, too." She leaned over the desk. "She also said he ordered running shorts for all the vets. She said he's done wonders for sales at the store and hopes he stays a long time. Anyway, the shorts should be here tomorrow and I wasn't to tell anyone, but…oops," she added as she realized she was doing exactly that.

"When did he do that? Buy the shorts?"

"Day before yesterday I think."

Susan was flabbergasted. Just when she wanted to kick him where the sun didn't shine, he was out doing something nice for her vets. They *had* looked like a raggedy bunch while running.

Were the running shorts a going-away present? He had more than a week left with them. Or was he going to just disappear after they'd invested their trust in him? No emotional investment on his part. Can't hurt if you don't care, and he really worked at that.

She decided to go to the ranch after all. Would he leave after they gave him the hat? Perhaps, if he felt he was getting too close to them, or they to him?

She drove to New Beginnings and looked for Danny. He was in the stables with Hobo.

"You missed the run," Danny said as Hobo limped over to her. "They'll be back soon. Ross added another half mile to the run."

"I heard he was hurt," she said.

"He was limping a little but then he took off with the others. Did you hear we got him a hat?"

"I did," she said. "That was great of you."

"We don't want him to leave,"

"A little bribery, huh?"

Not that it would work. He was determined to be the Lone Ranger. She suddenly wanted to get away. "I'm going to take Brandy for a ride. I know Lisa's at the clinic today and Brandy needs some exercise."

Danny looked a little surprised but nodded.

She saddled Brandy and mounted her. As she rode away from the barn, she saw the runners returning. It was a strange-looking sight as they jogged down a country road wearing cowboy hats and clothes ranging from running shorts to jeans. They were bunched closer than before. No stragglers today.

She pressed Brandy into a trot as she puzzled why she'd even come here this morning. Maybe her pride didn't want him to know how he'd crushed her last night. She'd trusted too easily, too fast. Again.

She sent Brandy into a gallop. She needed to feel the wind in her hair, the sun on her face. These were her mountains, her town, her friends.

Forget Ross Taylor.

She headed toward the lake where she used to go to parties long before Josh purchased the land. The former owners had built a log cabin there for visiting relatives and for community get-togethers.

Susan reached the lake and dismounted. It was a fine morning. The sun was reflected in the water. A cool breeze drifted through the pines, filling the air with their scent.

How could she have been so foolish to fall so quickly for a man she knew so little about? Apparently, she was a slow learner.

She found a stone and started skimming it along the surface of the lake and watching the ripples.

Brandy neighed. Susan looked up and saw a rider approach. From his height and the large horse he was riding, she knew exactly who it was. She stood, ready to mount Brandy again. But she didn't want him to think she was running from him.

Susan just didn't want to be in the same space with him. She was too darn attracted to him, even now, more fool her.

He dismounted and limped slightly as he neared her.

"What happened?" she asked.

"You haven't heard?"

"Bits and pieces." She shook her head. "You chose the police chief to run into? And at the Rusty Nail?"

"Rather embarrassing... No, it was definitely humiliating."

"You don't look too damaged."

"A few cuts. I was lucky." He paused, then added, "I was kicking myself for being an idiot and had a beer. Clint was turning into the parking lot, and I was leaving. I swerved to miss him and fell."

He had her attention. "And..."

"We agreed both of us were somewhat at fault."

He looked fairly undamaged. "You were running this morning," she accused him in her coolest voice.

"I did. I didn't want my leg to stiffen up. It's no big deal."

She changed the subject. "How did you know I was here?" she demanded.

"I didn't," Ross replied. "Josh brought me here a few days ago and it seemed a quiet place to flay myself. It wasn't you last night that made me back off. It was me.

I have my demons, and I was afraid they would affect you. It turns out they couldn't do any worse than I did.

"The simplest explanation," he said slowly, "is I didn't trust myself. I've never known permanence except the army and that's a damn poor example of permanence."

He led his horse to the porch of the cabin and sat on its edge. She hesitated, then followed. She sensed she was not going to like what he was trying to say.

"My father hung himself when I was ten," he said finally. "I found him in the barn. It was a stormy night before the bank was to take over our ranch. My mother had spent the day packing. I'd spent it saying goodbye to my horse and dog. We couldn't take them with us and I loved them as only a small, lonely boy can.

"I hadn't been able to sleep. I had to go see Bandit, my horse, one last time. When I opened the door, the gusts of wind sent his body swinging on a rope tied to a support beam. My mother was none too stable before that night and after his suicide, she drank heavily and then just disappeared."

His voice had turned robotic, as though telling it that way would keep emotion at bay. But she felt it. Felt the pain of that young boy. Her hand crept over and took his, her fingers entwining with his. She had questions but she wasn't going to interrupt him. She'd sensed something behind his restlessness, but this was far worse than she'd imagined. She knew now why he'd hesitated at the door of the barn on his first day at the ranch.

His hand tightened around hers. "I was passed around by her relatives," he continued. "None of them had much money and I was just an added financial burden. I got to where I never unpacked my suitcase because I didn't know where I would be the next night.

"I joined the army the day I graduated from high school, which led to my current career. To me it meant independence. I would never have to rely on any individual or organization again."

Ross continued, "That defensive instinct struck last night. If you don't care, you don't get hurt. If you don't depend on anyone, they can never disappoint you. I... care about you too much," he added after a short silence. "My defensive instincts sprung up."

"But you *do* care. I've seen it with the vets."

"That's temporary. Same with other patients I have. I help them temporarily. I don't invest myself in them."

"Yes, you do," she said. "I've seen you invest yourself in every veteran here. It's part of you, even if you don't want to admit it."

"But then I can leave. There's no long-term responsibility. I can't hurt anyone. They can't hurt me." He paused, then added, "Until now."

He reached over and kissed her. It was slow and steaming and thick with emotion. "I don't want to lose you. I didn't last night, either, which is why I unwisely went running to a bar and ran into a police car," he added ruefully. "Not a great example for our vets."

She had to smile then. He looked chagrined, like a boy caught smoking behind a garage. She leaned against his body and kissed him lightly. No demands. "And you. How much damage did you do to yourself?"

"Not as much as I deserved, but it hurt like hell," he added. "It improved when I saw you."

"I was trying to avoid you," she admitted.

He leaned over and his fingers stroked the side of her neck in gentle movements. "I was an ass."

"You were," she agreed, but the hurt and anger drained

from her as he traced patterns on her face and then reached over and kissed her as if she would break.

Sensation—wonderful, betraying waves of sensation—swept over her as the kiss deepened. All she wanted was to continue, to see where it would carry her. She closed her eyes to better lose herself in the feelings created by his touch. His lips were gentle, unexpectedly gentle, then she felt them tighten against hers with a desperate need she now understood and reciprocated. Both of them had been hiding from their pasts.

She opened her eyes, feeling pleasure in seeing his face so close, so intent, so strong in its rugged, uncompromising planes.

A sense of well-being washed over her as his arms tightened around her and held her close. His lips brushed hers lightly as if asking permission to proceed. As his hands ran over her, she felt her soul singing and her body was the chorus.

It was insane. They were in the open and nearly tearing clothes off one another. "Here?" she asked.

He looked dazed but didn't let go. "Probably not," he said, "but I wanted to do that since I first met you."

"I couldn't tell," she said.

"I've always been able to stonewall my feelings," he replied. "Until now." His steel-gray gaze appeared to soften as he studied her. "You're so damned irresistible," he said.

She didn't know what to stay to that. She just leaned against him, feeling his strength, yet now sensing a vulnerability that made her heart ache. Her arms went around his neck and she stretched upward until their bodies fit together. She wanted more of the sensations rocking her body and the emotions shimmering between them. Desire spread throughout her like a summer's sun pooling...

He groaned. "Not here," he said. "I don't have...any protection."

"And I'm not on the pill," she replied. "We should go back. We...you...will be missed."

"Later then?" he asked.

"You won't drive into a police car again?"

He looked chastened. "No."

"Okay. What time?"

"Around five? I'm meeting with Sam Martin at four. Where?"

"The inn. I'm usually there anyway."

"Won't people talk?"

"After last night at the falls, I think they probably already are."

He raised an eyebrow.

"I'm a grown woman," she said. "And Mark is very discreet."

They met again that night at the inn.

They'd gone through the rest of the morning trying not to look at each other. It didn't work. Vets and instructors were watching, smiling, snickering at their pathetic attempts to look in any direction other than each other.

Susan gave up at noon and drove to her cottage, where she fed Vagabond and sat down to have a discussion with the cat. *Could she really trust Ross? Would he just pick up and leave next week? Could you really fall in love so quickly?*

Unfortunately, Vagabond had no answers although she seemed to sympathize. She rubbed against Susan's legs and meowed softly with rare affection.

At fifteen to five, she walked to the inn as she often did. Ross's bike was parked near the side door. She went inside and knocked softly at his door.

When he opened it, they didn't say anything. Just reached for each other before he pulled her inside.

Their lips met with such tender wistfulness that Ross felt a bliss that surpassed any feeling he'd known before. It filled him, cleansed him, renewed him. He'd felt pleasure before: pride at finishing his doctorate, triumph when a patient healed, satisfaction as he watched his vets ride their horses with confidence, but he'd never felt joy like this. Now he knew, and he was a glutton.

It was only a few days since they'd met but he felt he knew her better than anyone he'd met. He knew her heart, and she knew his faults and was still here. His fingers teased as he slipped off her blouse and bra. They roamed against the back of her neck, then explored the rest of her.

He didn't question now that he was going too fast. He knew to the bottom of his soul that it was right, had been right since the moment they met. He'd always scorned love at first sight. Never again.

"We'll take it slow," he said.

"I don't think so," she replied.

He leaned over and kissed her slowly as his arms tightened around her, then his lips explored her body, teasing and loving.

He'd been waiting for this all his life, only he hadn't known it.

"It's so fast," he whispered, offering her a chance to back away.

"It happens," she replied. "Travis and Jenny…they knew in five days, and they're as in love with each other as the day they married." She paused, then whispered,

"I'm not afraid. I was, but not now." Her hand went up to his face, traced its outlines with tender possessiveness.

His hands moved over her body, igniting increasingly urgent sensations. Susan heard her own moan, knew the longing of her body—or was it her soul—to make love with him.

The friction of their bodies was no longer enough. She was consumed with feeling and wanting more. "Ross," she uttered, knowing it was more a gasp than a word.

His lips left her mouth, moved to her ear, where he nibbled on it, sending shivers of pleasure through her. His feathering kisses moved to her neck, to the pulse of her throat. Her eyes misted as she felt the tenderness in each caress, the tethered need in each touch. She felt his body shudder with restraint even as its rigidity radiated his need.

She wanted to give him everything—laughter, sweetness, joy. She wanted to watch him smile.

"I did get some protection," he whispered as he finished undressing her, then she did the same to him. He lifted her easily and gently lowered her to the bed. He leaned down and his mouth met hers. Shivers of pleasure rolled through her body even as her heart hammered against her rib cage.

"Are you sure, Susan?" he asked.

"Never more so," she replied, surprising herself with the words, but she'd never felt as alive as she did this moment. She wanted him as much as he obviously wanted her.

Her hands touched his chest, playing with the patterns of his muscles, with the arrow of hair that ran down toward his arousal. Her heart was a bass drum now as he lowered himself over her. His hands went under her hips and she felt him tease her gently. He probed at first, then slowly, enticingly he entered her, moving sensuously. Her body moved to the rhythm of his in a dance that grew in intensity and tempo. Her legs went around his, bringing him even farther into her as her body built to a crescendo of sensations. Her body continued to feel waves of pleasure as he pulled out of her, rolled next to her and held her.

"Wow," she said. It was all she could manage at the moment.

"Yeah," he said, "Wow." He paused, then asked, "How long were you engaged before you married what's his name?"

"Four months and then married two years before I came to my senses," she said slowly.

"I'm a bad risk too, you know," he said as he played with her fingers. "I have a host of ghosts running around inside my head. I'm used to doing everything my way. I like motorcycles and I run into police cars."

"It means I have a lot of work to do."

He nodded. "No doubt."

She stared at him and slowly smiled.

"We should get married soon," he continued.

"I don't think you've asked me yet?" she pointed out.

"Will you consider it?" he ventured.

"You're loco," she observed.

"Now, that is insulting," he said with a slight smile. "But it seems like we have two choices. We can sneak around and be the talk of the town, or we can get married."

"Engagement is an option and I thought you were going on that road trip."

"A very short engagement is acceptable," he said.

"Jubal offered to lease me that piece of land in the back of his property and I'm certain I can get an option to buy."

"He did?" She couldn't hide her surprise.

"I think he wants to make a permanent cowboy out of me, with the help of our veterans. Sort of a backup to Luke."

"You're still loco, particularly about marrying me. We don't even know each other."

"I know all the important stuff." He shrugged. "You're smart. You're one of the kindest people I've ever met, and you're sexy as hell. A potent combination I don't want to get away.

"And," he added, "you know me better than people I've known for decades." He paused, looked thoughtful and added, "One of my buddies—a fighter pilot on an aircraft carrier—was on leave. He was on a bus when he saw a woman on the street. Never seen her before. He jumped off the bus, accosted her and told her he was going to marry her."

"Did she call the police?"

"Nope. She married him before his leave was up, which was five days. He was also a brave man. Her father was a prison warden. I didn't believe him until his wife swore it was true."

She narrowed her eyes. "For how long? Were they married, I mean?"

"Twenty years and still going."

She gave him a suspicious look.

"It's the truth," he swore. "You'll probably meet them someday."

"Are you sure you want to live on a ranch? You don't liked barns or stables," she pointed out.

"I'm learning to," he said, suddenly serious. "I like

riding. I like horses. I have been thinking about accepting Josh's offer. I've never had a real home, even the ranch when I was a kid. My…parents were always fighting.

"I feel more at home here in a few days than I've felt anywhere. I have friends here. I can still take PT jobs in the area. Maybe I've reached the point where I can stop running from the past."

"You're really serious," she said, her eyes wide.

He nodded. "I am. I see how happy Josh, Jubal and the others are. I really like working with the vets."

"A Colorado cowboy? I like it. You looked good in your new hat."

"It means a lot to me," he said. "More than any gift I've received. Except for you." On that note, he kissed her, long and passionately. "I want to do a lot of that."

"Are you reneging on one week?"

"Hell no."

"Make it a month," she countered.

"Or sooner," he bargained.

"Or sooner," she agreed and sealed the bargain with a very long kiss.

Epilogue

Susan and Ross were married several weeks later, on the last day of the current New Beginnings program. The participants in the program were the guests of honor.

It was a small but rowdy wedding. The fourteen special guests all wore their cowboy hats and were joined by the other members of the Covenant Falls veteran community and their wives.

Susan wore a simple blue dress with flowers entwined in her hair. Ross wore new jeans and a Western shirt and his wedding present from Jubal: a pair of riding boots. The minister came from the town's Baptist church.

It was a beautiful fall day. A breeze rippled the lake surface and the sun blessed the mountain above them. Ross's heart beat faster as he looked at Susan's face as they said their vows. She was incredibly beautiful.

Her eyes glistened as she gave him a smile meant only for him.

As they finished the ceremony, he heard the neigh of horses behind him. Most of the guests rode horses to the lake, and their mounts apparently wanted to participate, as did Hobo, who trailed down the aisle with him. Unfortunately, Vagabond did not lower herself enough to attend and was brooding in the cabin. The two, though, had come to an understanding: they ignored one another. But both Susan and Ross believed they would become buddies. Eventually.

The ceremony finished and they were embraced by old and new friends. Food and drink were bountiful. Heartfelt goodbyes were said as the program's vets were leaving in the morning.

Finally, it was just the four of them. Ross and Susan, Hobo and Vagabond. Their horses were being taken to Jubal's barn and would appear the next morning. Ross planned to build a small stable next to the cabin now that he had closed on the property a week earlier.

After all the guests left, Ross and Susan stayed outside on the porch, their hands locked together, and watched the sun set.

She took his hand. "No more shadows?" she asked.

"No." He swallowed hard. He had arrived in Covenant Falls a loner leery of commitments. Now he had an enchanting wife, an entire town of friends, a dog, a cat, even Cajun he was buying from Jubal.

As a kid—before his world fell apart—he'd wanted to be a cowboy.

Life took him on a long winding road to get here but now here he was. A bona fide Colorado cowboy with a horse, a hat and a wife who'd made it all happen.

As if reading his mind, his new wife leaned over and kissed him with such gusto he believed they should retire inside. And they did.

* * * * *

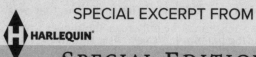
When Matt looked up, she offered him a shy smile. "Like I said, I'm sorry. I should have told you that you were a father."

"You've got that right."

"I've made mistakes, but Emily isn't one of them. She's a great kid. So for now, let's focus on her."

"All right." Matt uncrossed his arms and raked a hand through his hair. "But just for the record, I would've done anything in my power to take care of you and Emily."

"I know." And that was why she'd walked away from him. Matt would have stood up to her father, challenged his threat, only to be knocked to his knees—and worse.

No, leaving town and cutting all ties with Matt was the only thing she could've done to protect him.

HSEEXP0519

As she stood in the room where their daughter was conceived, as she studied the only man she'd ever loved, the memories crept up on her…the old feelings, too.

When she was sixteen, there'd been something about the fun-loving nineteen-year-old cowboy that had drawn her attention. And whatever it was continued to tug at her now. But she shook it off. Too many years had passed; too many tears had been shed.

Besides, an unwed single mother who was expecting another man's baby wouldn't stand a chance with a champion bull rider who had his choice of pretty cowgirls. And she'd best not forget that.

"Aw, hell," Matt said, as he ran a hand through his hair again and blew out a weary sigh. "Maybe you did Emily a favor by leaving when you did. Who knows what kind of father I would have made back then. Or even now."

Don't miss
The Cowboy's Secret Family *by Judy Duarte,*
available June 2019 wherever
Harlequin® Special Edition books and ebooks are sold.

www.Harlequin.com

Need an adrenaline rush from nail-biting tales
(and irresistible males)?

Check out **Harlequin Intrigue®**,
Harlequin® Romantic Suspense and
Love Inspired® Suspense books!

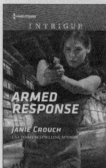  

New books available every month!

CONNECT WITH US AT:

**ROMANCE WHEN
YOU NEED IT**

SGENRE2018R

Looking for more satisfying love stories
with community and family at their core?

Check out **Harlequin® Special Edition**
and **Love Inspired®** books!

New books available every month!

CONNECT WITH US AT:

Facebook.com/groups/HarlequinConnection

Facebook.com/HarlequinBooks

Twitter.com/HarlequinBooks

Instagram.com/HarlequinBooks

Pinterest.com/HarlequinBooks

ReaderService.com

**ROMANCE WHEN
YOU NEED IT**

HFGENRE2018

Reward the book lover in you!

Earn points on your purchase of new Harlequin books from participating retailers.

Turn your points into **FREE BOOKS** of your choice!

Join for FREE today at
www.HarlequinMyRewards.com.

Harlequin My Rewards is a free program (no fees) without any commitments or obligations.

MYR18